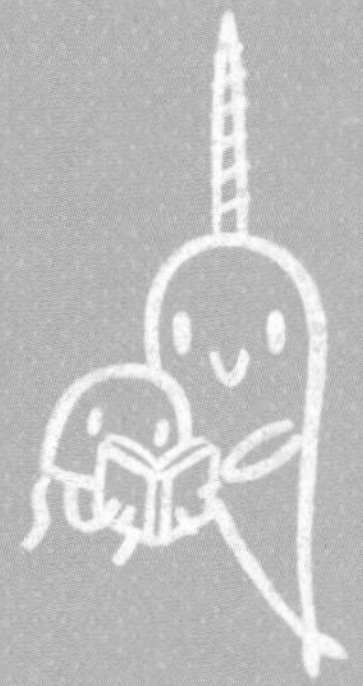

HAVE YOU READ THESE
NARWHAL AND JELLY BOOKS?

NARWHAL: UNICORN OF THE SEA!

SUPER NARWHAL AND JELLY JOLT

PEANUT BUTTER AND JELLY

NARWHAL'S OTTER FRIEND

HAPPY NARWHALIDAYS

NARWHAL'S SCHOOL OF AWESOMENESS

NARWHALICORN

AND JELLY

BEN CLANTON

tundra

to Olicorn!

Tundra Books, an imprint of Tundra Book Group,
a division of Penguin Random House of Canada Limited

Library and Archives Canada Cataloguing in Publication

Title: Narwhalicorn and Jelly / Ben Clanton.
Names: Clanton, Ben, 1988- author, illustrator.
Series: Clanton, Ben, 1988- Narwhal and Jelly book.
Description: Series statement: A Narwhal and Jelly book ; 7
Identifiers: Canadiana (print) 20210335963 | Canadiana (ebook) 20210335971 |
ISBN 9780735266728 (hardcover) | ISBN 9780735266735 (EPUB)
Subjects: LCGFT: Graphic novels.
Classification: LCC PZ7.C523 Nar 2022 | DDC j741.5/973—dc23

Published simultaneously in the United States of America by Tundra Books of Northern New York,
an imprint of Tundra Book Group, a division of Penguin Random House of Canada Limited

Library of Congress Control Number: 2021948356

Edited by Tara Walker and Peter Phillips
Designed by Ben Clanton
The artwork in this book was rendered using mainly Procreate and Adobe Photoshop.
The text was set in a typeface based on hand-lettering by Ben Clanton.

Printed in Canada

www.penguinrandomhouse.ca

1   2   3   4   5   26   25   24   23   22

tundra | Penguin
Random House
TUNDRA BOOKS

CONTENTS

UNICORNS

NARWHALS
OF THE LAND

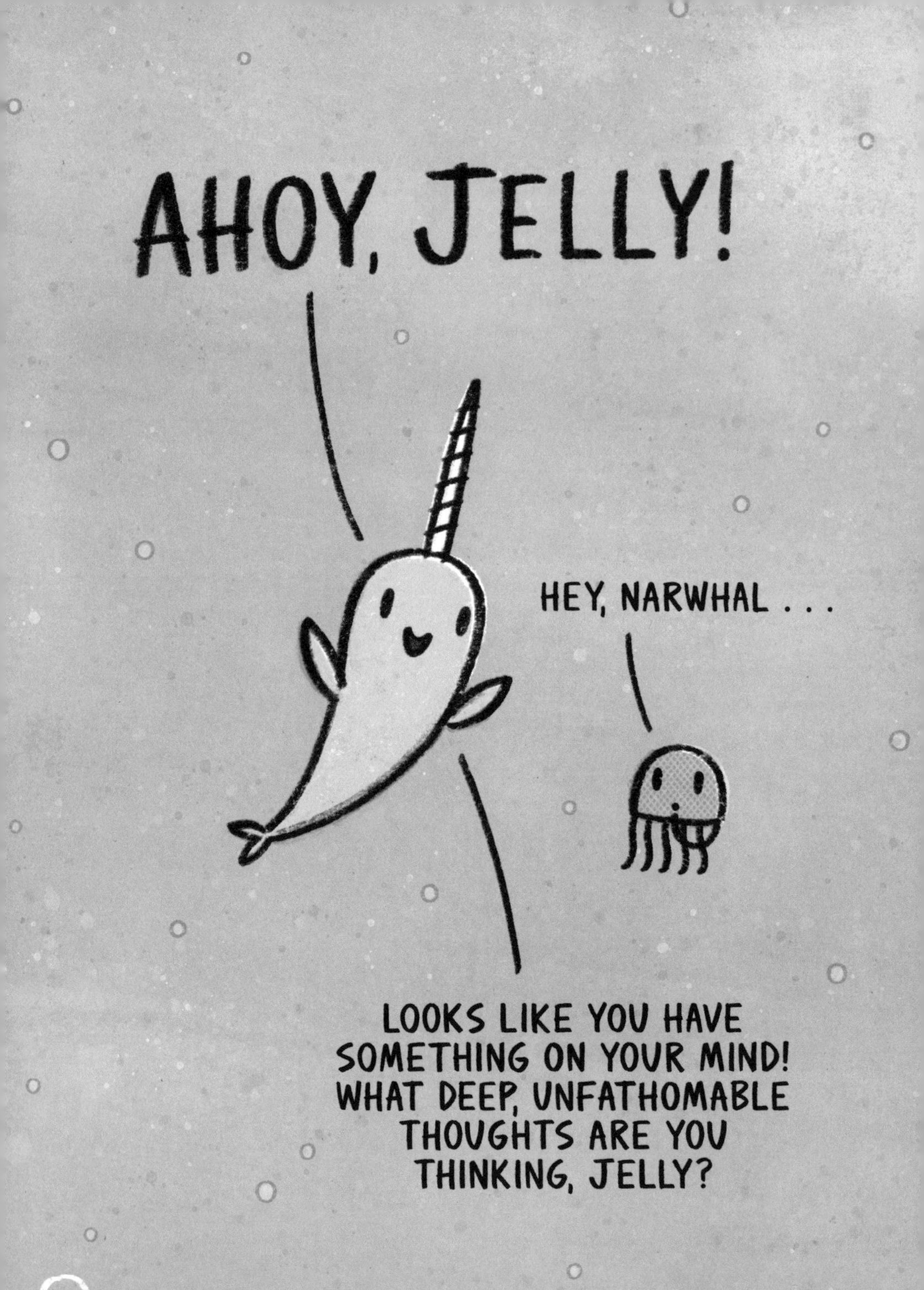
AHOY, JELLY!
HEY, NARWHAL . . .
LOOKS LIKE YOU HAVE SOMETHING ON YOUR MIND! WHAT DEEP, UNFATHOMABLE THOUGHTS ARE YOU THINKING, JELLY?

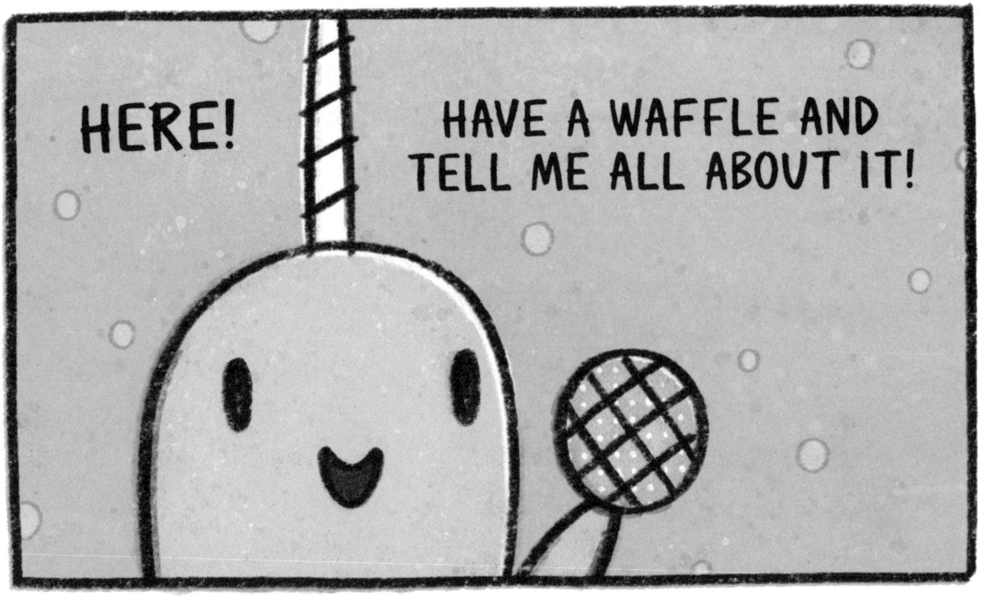
HERE!
HAVE A WAFFLE AND TELL ME ALL ABOUT IT!

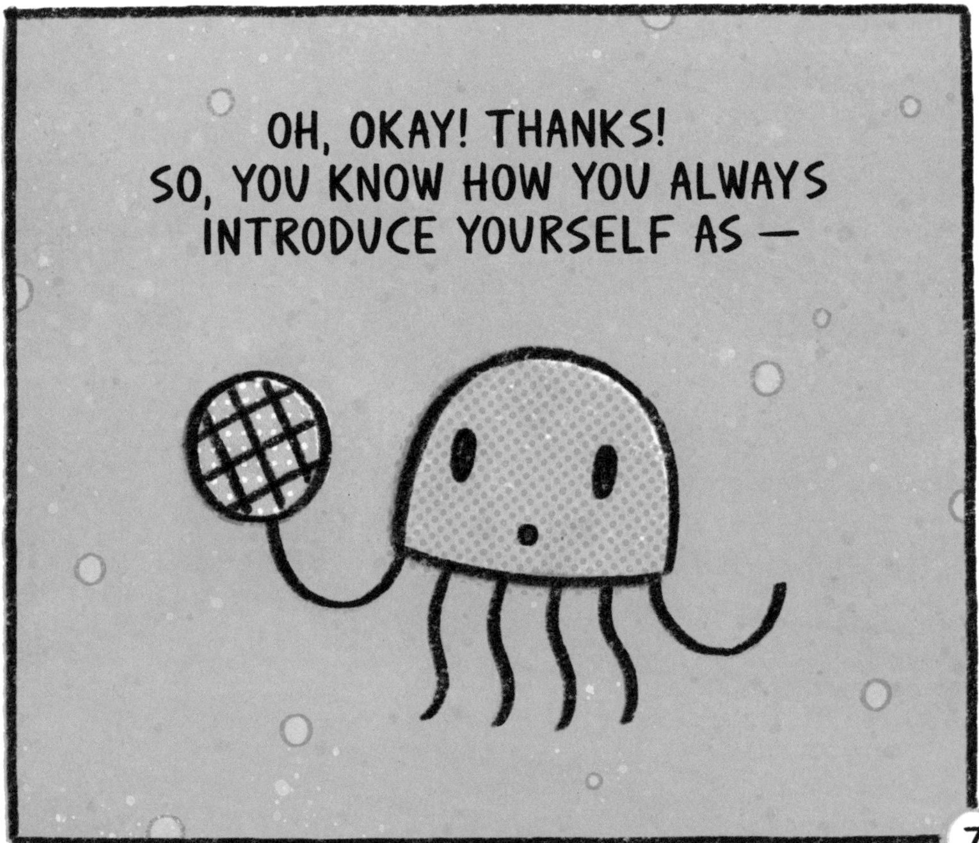
OH, OKAY! THANKS!
SO, YOU KNOW HOW YOU ALWAYS INTRODUCE YOURSELF AS —

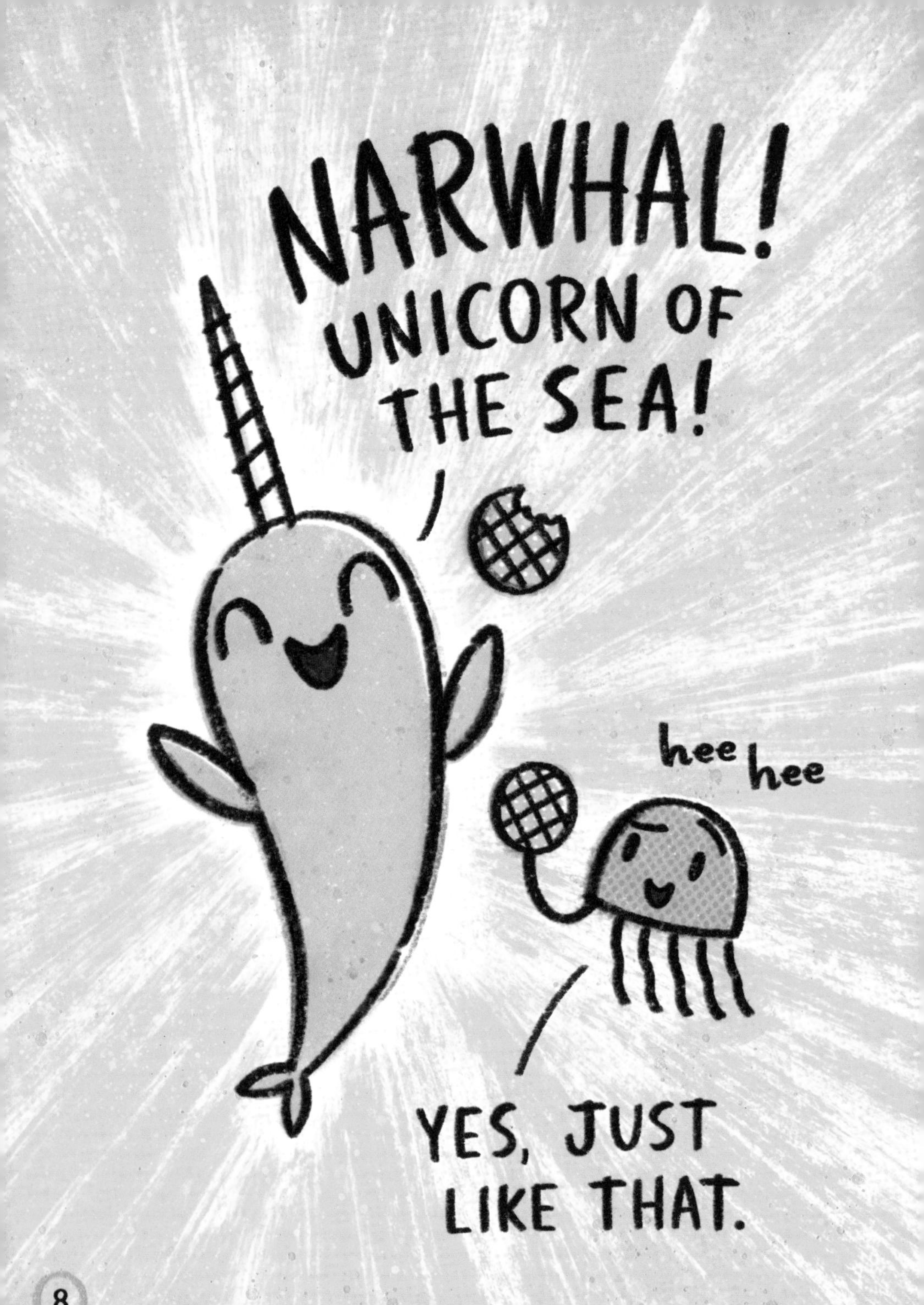
NARWHAL! UNICORN OF THE SEA!
hee hee
YES, JUST LIKE THAT.

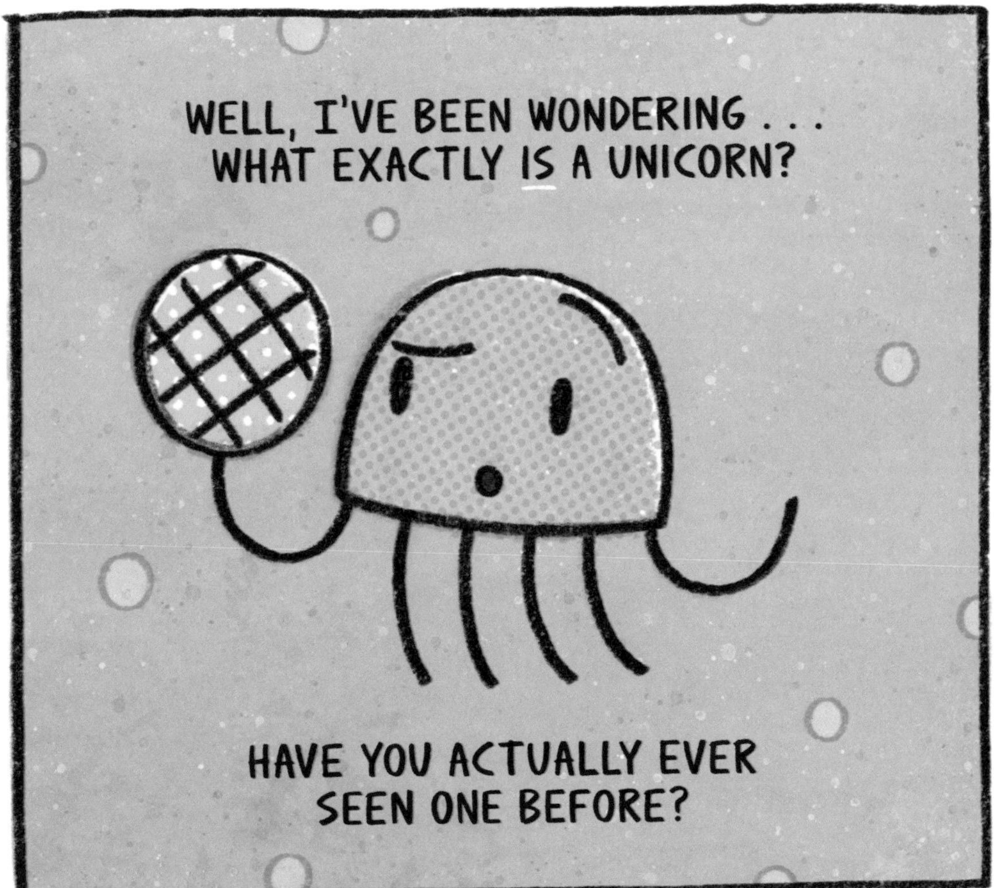
WELL, I'VE BEEN WONDERING . . .
WHAT EXACTLY IS A UNICORN?
HAVE YOU ACTUALLY EVER SEEN ONE BEFORE?

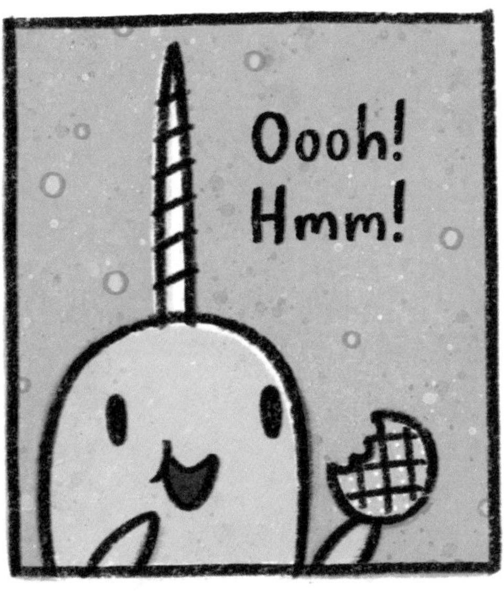
Oooh! Hmm!

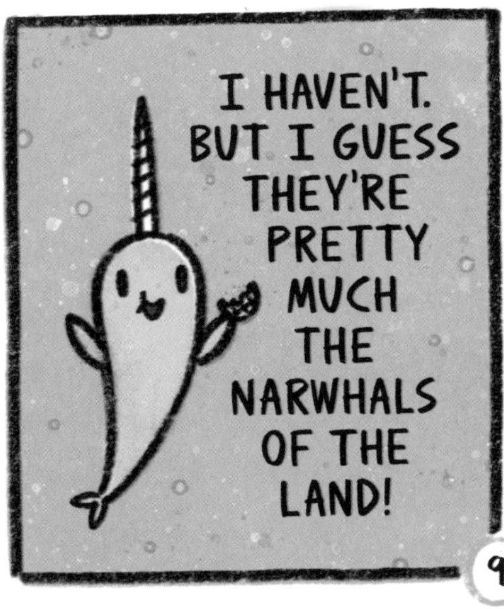
I HAVEN'T. BUT I GUESS THEY'RE PRETTY MUCH THE NARWHALS OF THE LAND!

SO, LIKE A NARWHAL WITH LONG, LANKY . . . WHAT DO THE LANDLUBBERS CALL THEM? PEGS?

SOMETHING LIKE THAT! IT SHORE WOULD BE SOMETHING TO WALK ON LAND AND SEE ONE!

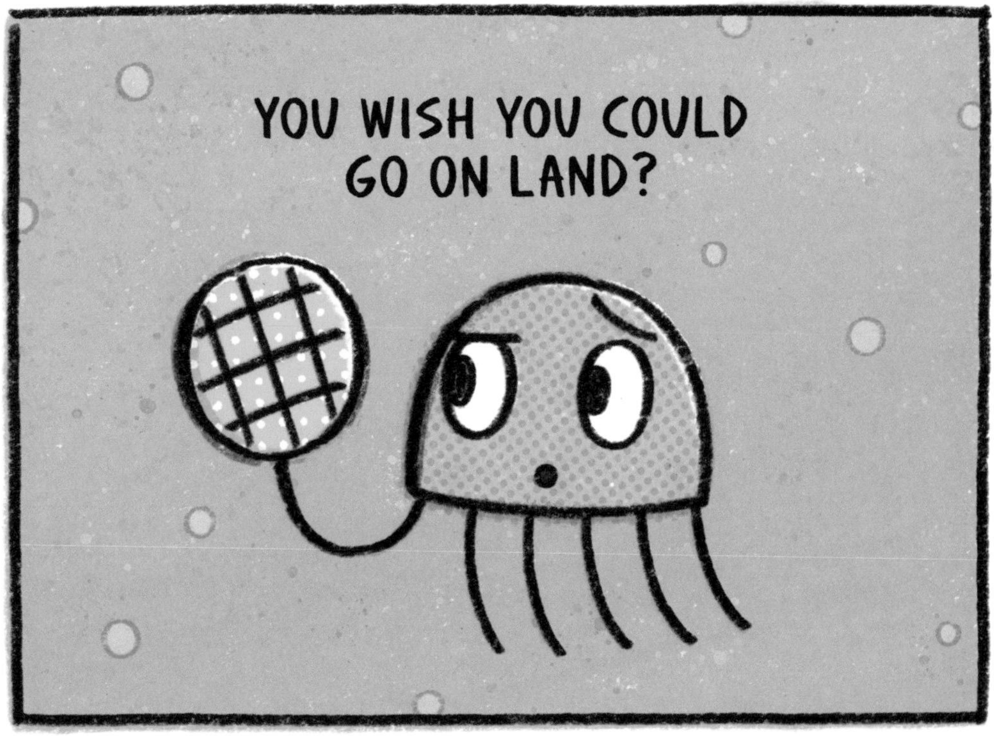
YOU WISH YOU COULD GO ON LAND?

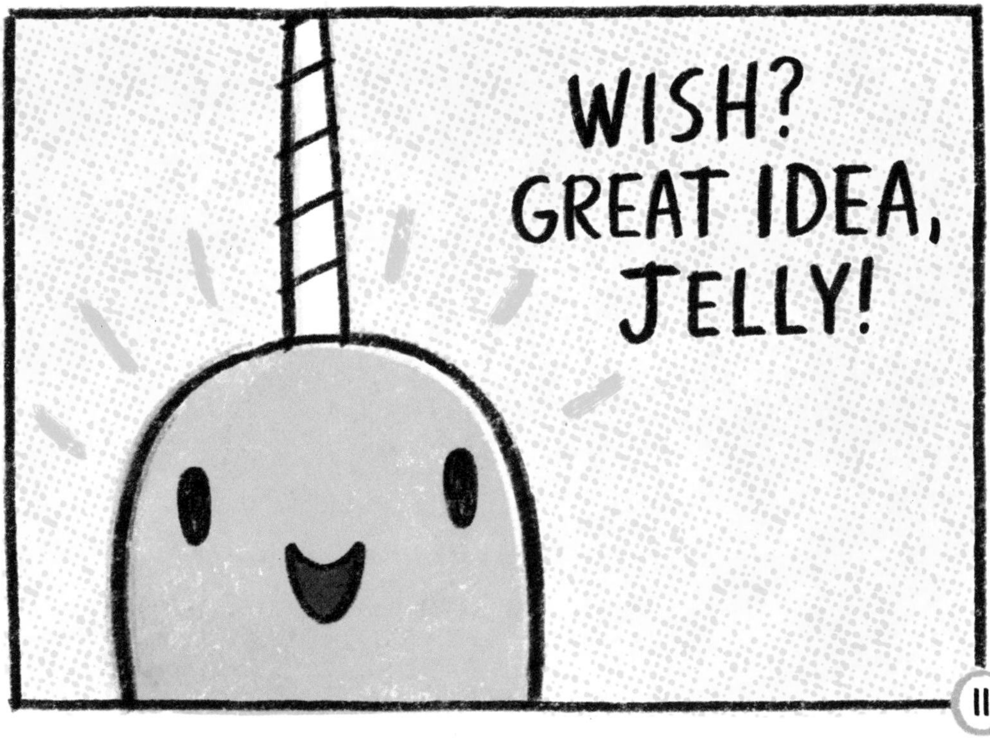
WISH? GREAT IDEA, JELLY!

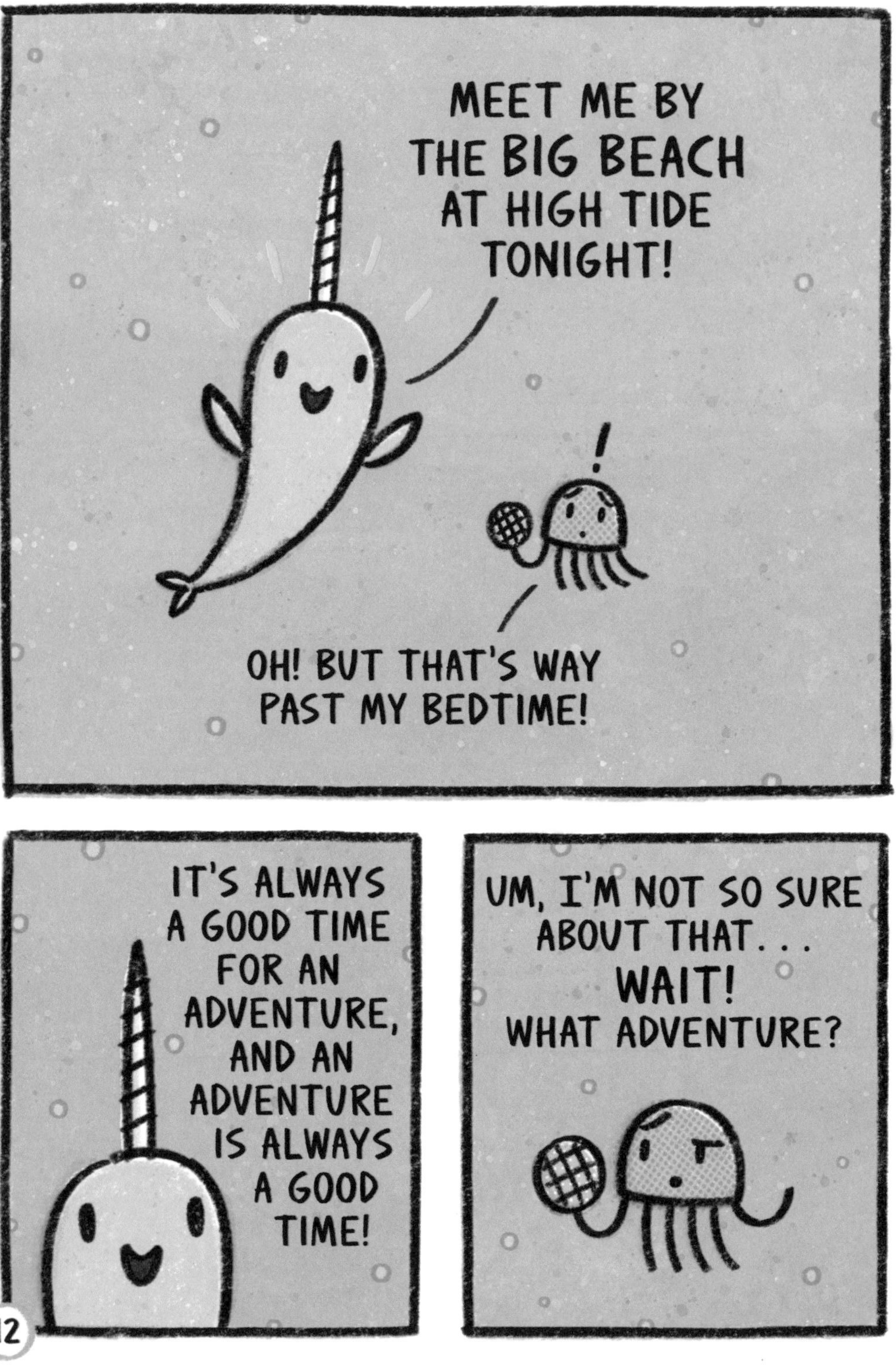
MEET ME BY THE BIG BEACH AT HIGH TIDE TONIGHT!
!
OH! BUT THAT'S WAY PAST MY BEDTIME!
IT'S ALWAYS A GOOD TIME FOR AN ADVENTURE, AND AN ADVENTURE IS ALWAYS A GOOD TIME!
UM, I'M NOT SO SURE ABOUT THAT. . . WAIT! WHAT ADVENTURE?

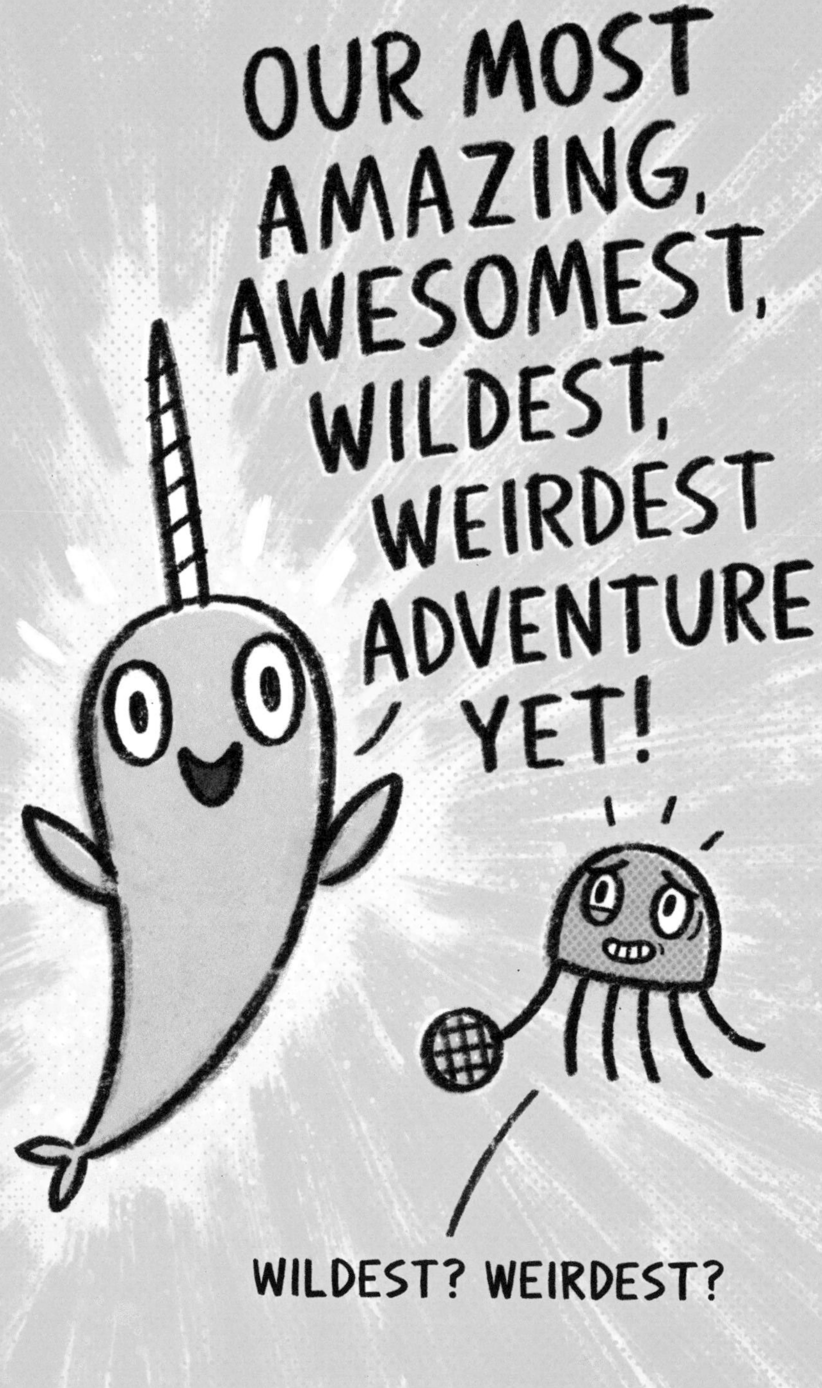
OUR MOST AMAZING, AWESOMEST, WILDEST, WEIRDEST ADVENTURE YET!
WILDEST? WEIRDEST?

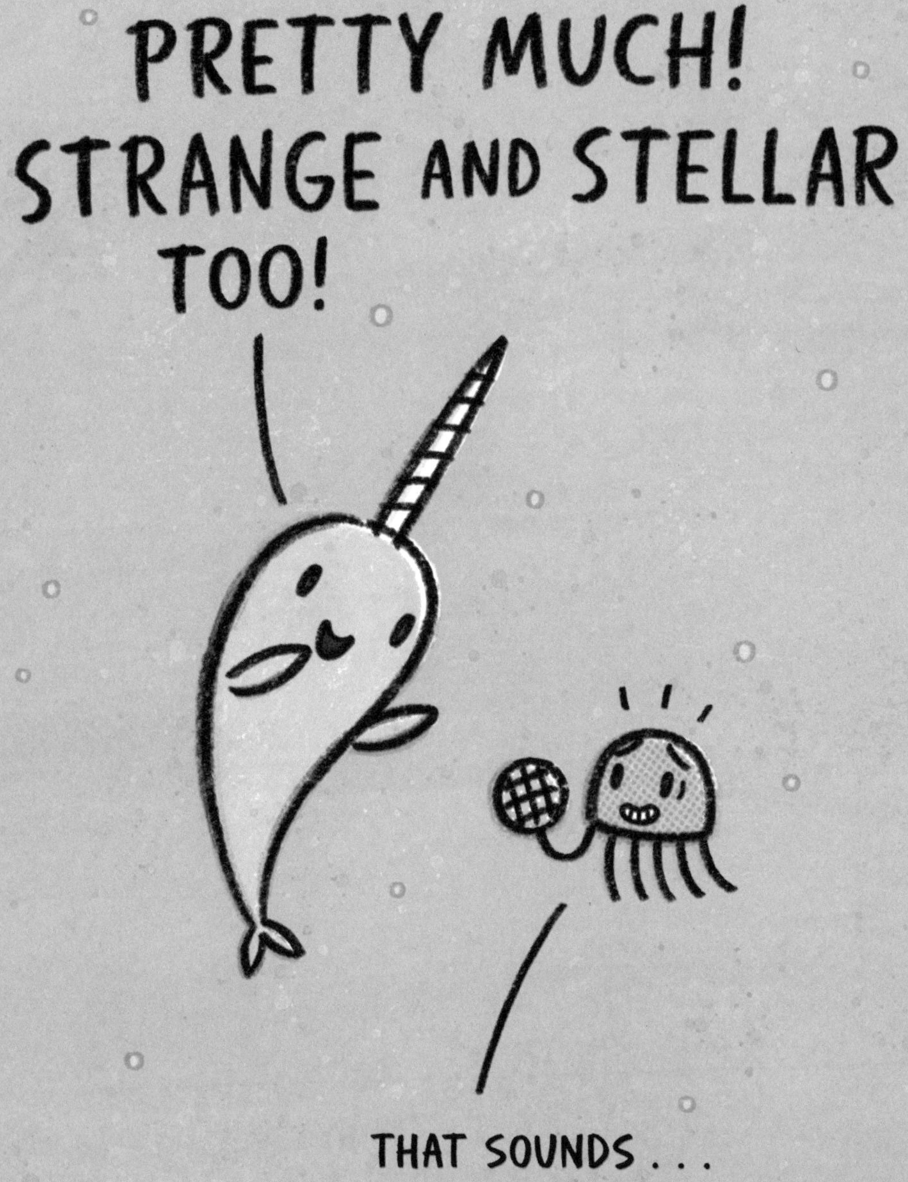
PRETTY MUCH! STRANGE AND STELLAR TOO!
THAT SOUNDS . . .

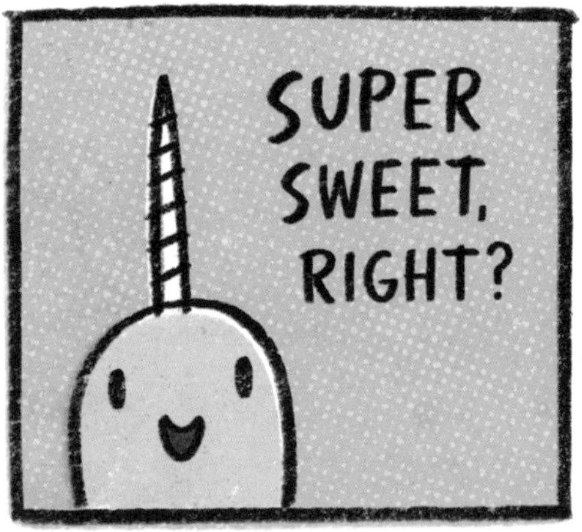
SUPER SWEET, RIGHT?

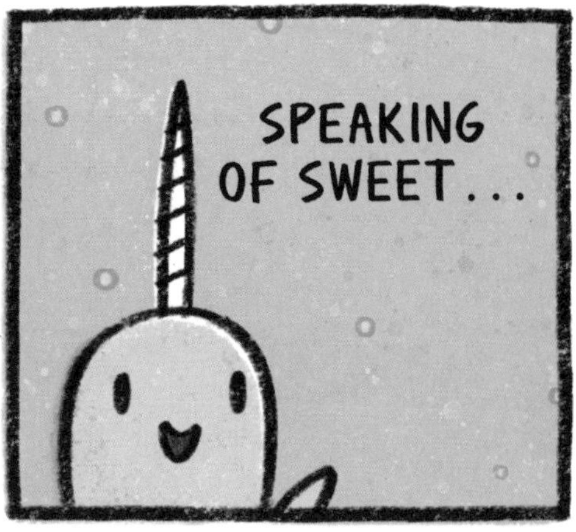
SPEAKING OF SWEET...

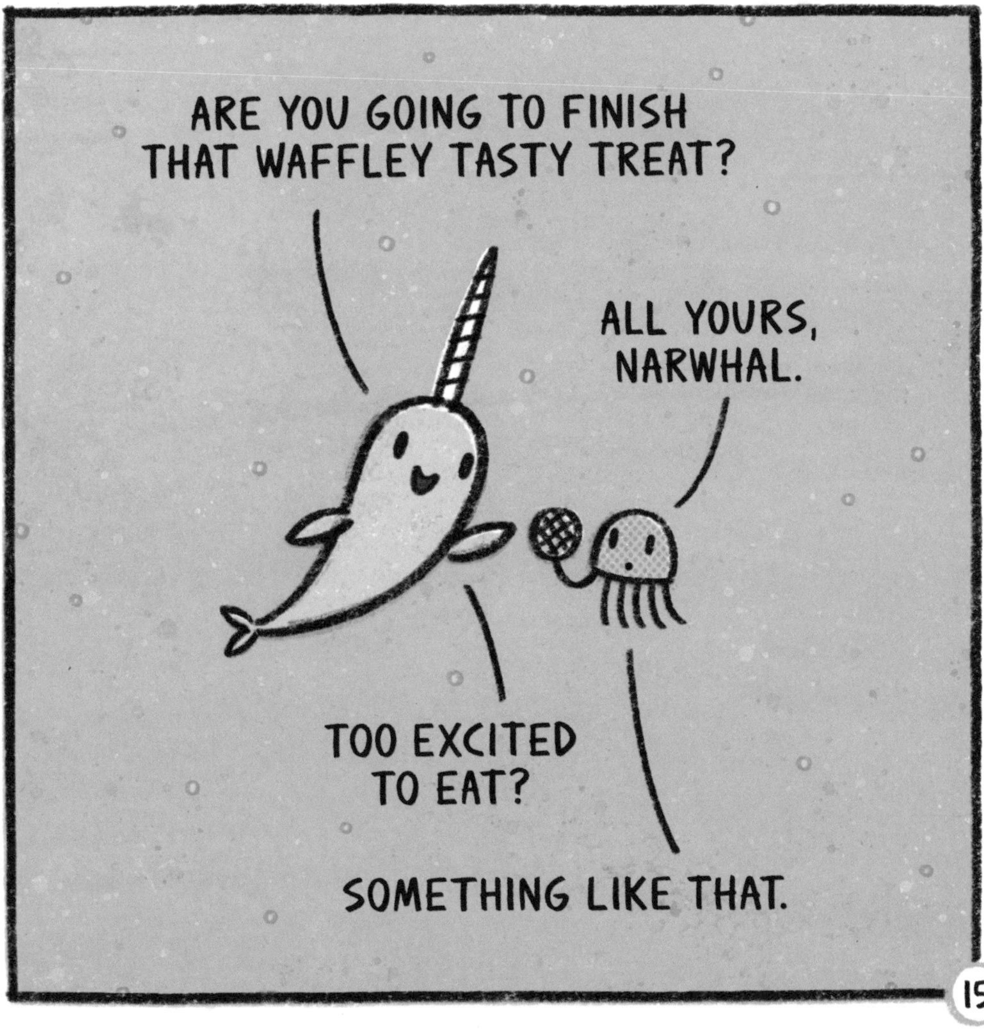
ARE YOU GOING TO FINISH THAT WAFFLEY TASTY TREAT?
ALL YOURS, NARWHAL.
TOO EXCITED TO EAT?
SOMETHING LIKE THAT.

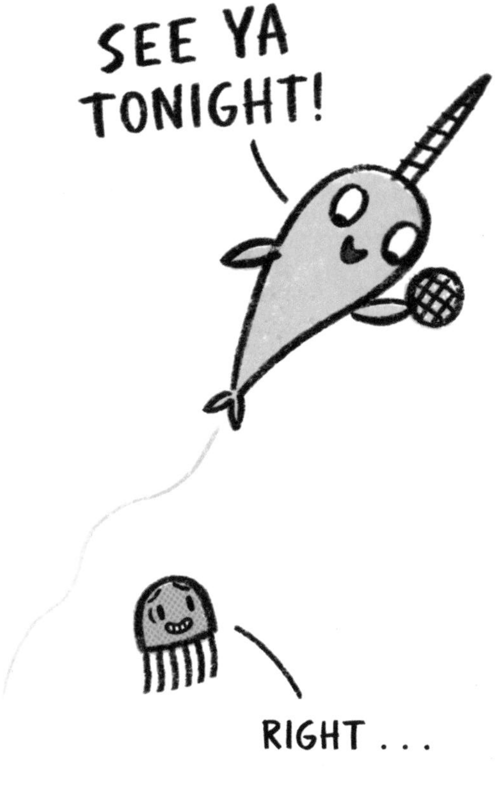
SEE YA TONIGHT!
RIGHT . . .

FUN FACTS
ABOUT REAL UNICORNS?

ELASMOTHERIUM (A.K.A. THE SIBERIAN UNICORN) IS AN EXTINCT TYPE OF RHINOCEROS THAT WAS SIMILAR IN SIZE TO A MAMMOTH AND HAD A HUGE HORN ON ITS FOREHEAD.

RHINO? I'M WOOLLY SOME SORT OF UNICORN!

NOT MUCH IS KNOWN ABOUT THE HORN-LIKE PROTRUSION OF UNICORNFISH.

WHAT I KNOW IS I LOOK AWESOME!

THE HUMMINGBIRD HAWK-MOTH HAS A "HORN" WHEN IT'S A LARVA!

BUT . . . IT ISN'T ON MY HEAD!

MORE UNIQUE UNICORNS?

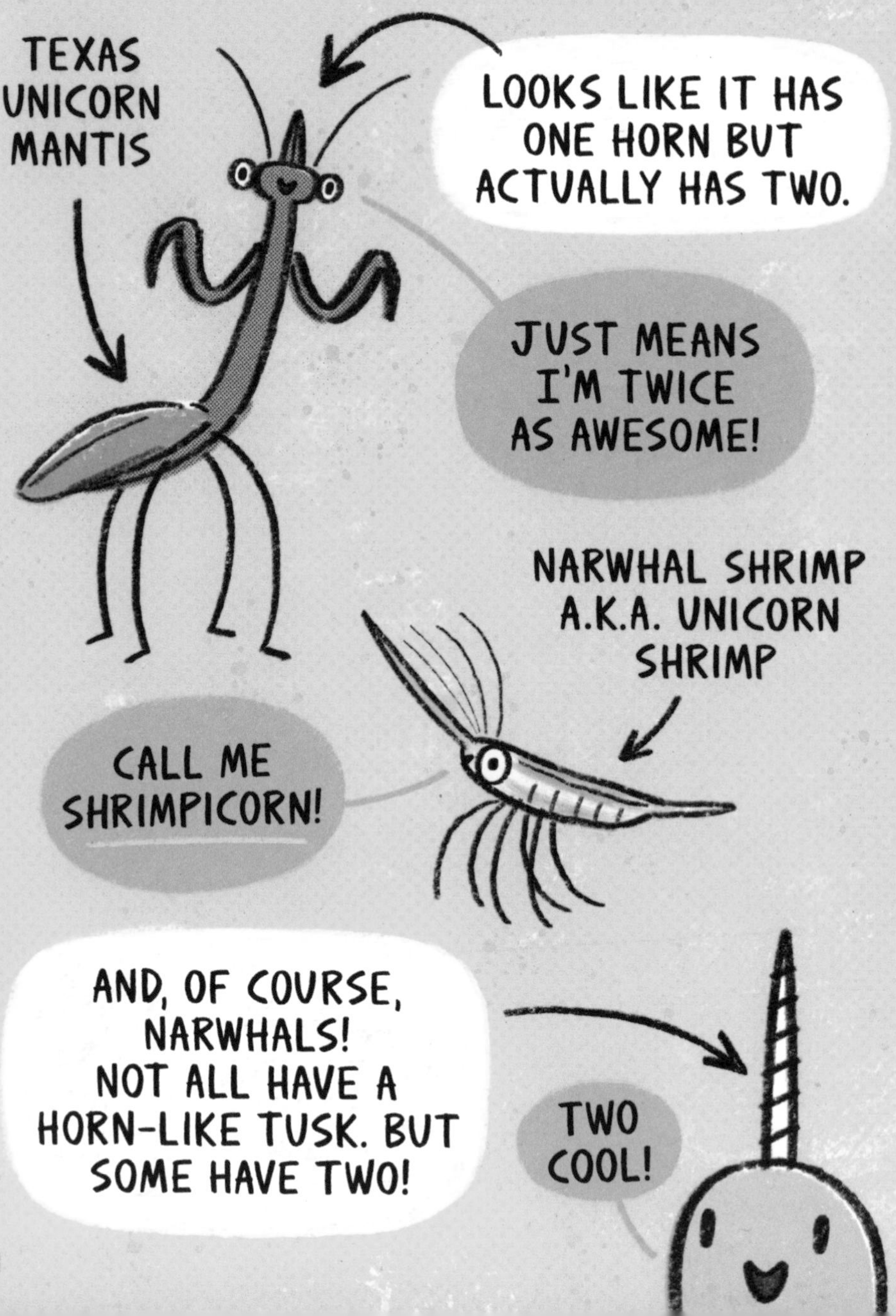
TEXAS UNICORN MANTIS
LOOKS LIKE IT HAS ONE HORN BUT ACTUALLY HAS TWO.
JUST MEANS I'M TWICE AS AWESOME!
NARWHAL SHRIMP A.K.A. UNICORN SHRIMP
CALL ME SHRIMPICORN!
AND, OF COURSE, NARWHALS! NOT ALL HAVE A HORN-LIKE TUSK. BUT SOME HAVE TWO!
TWO COOL!

HAVE THIS WISH
I FISH TONIGHT

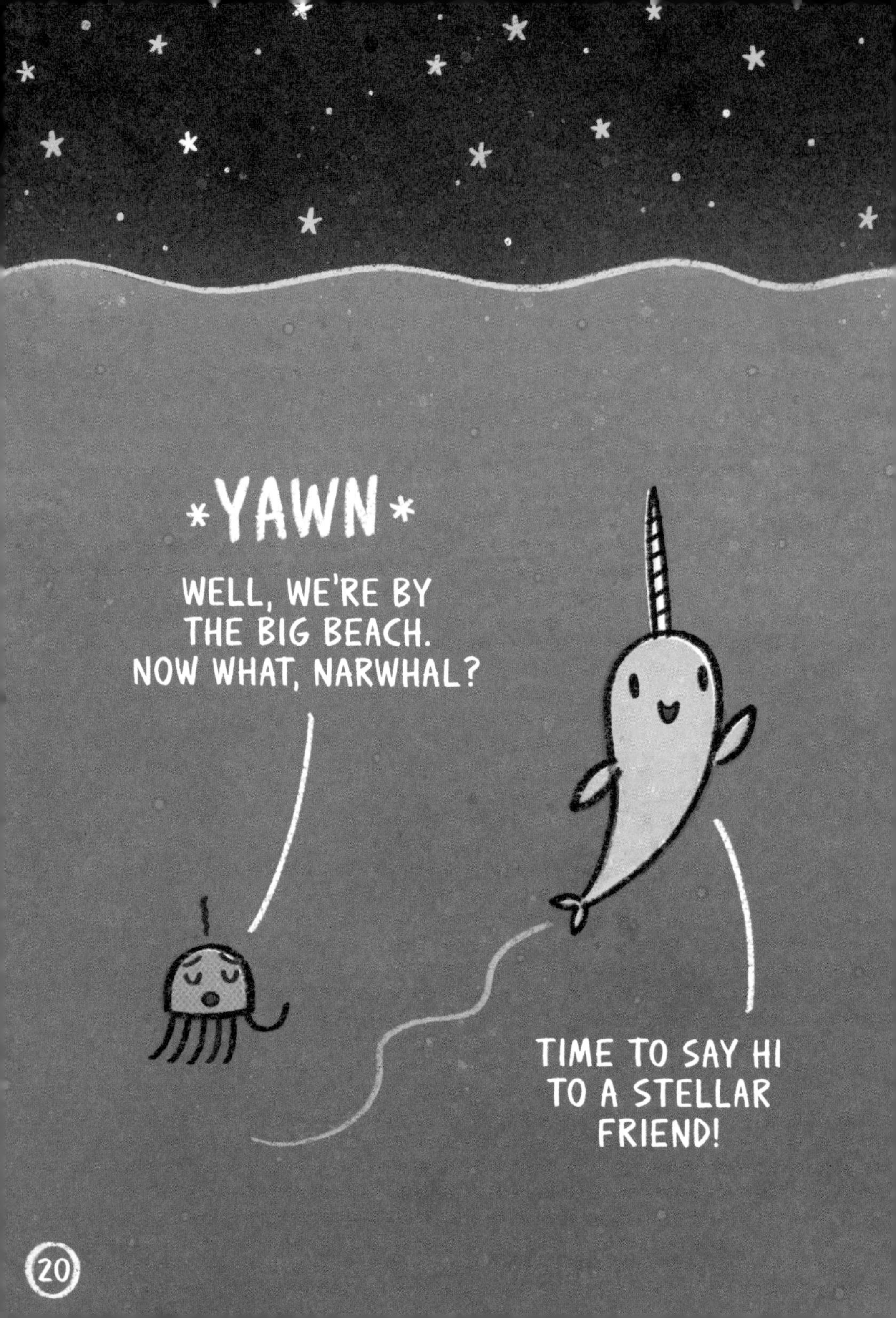
YAWN
WELL, WE'RE BY THE BIG BEACH. NOW WHAT, NARWHAL?
TIME TO SAY HI TO A STELLAR FRIEND!

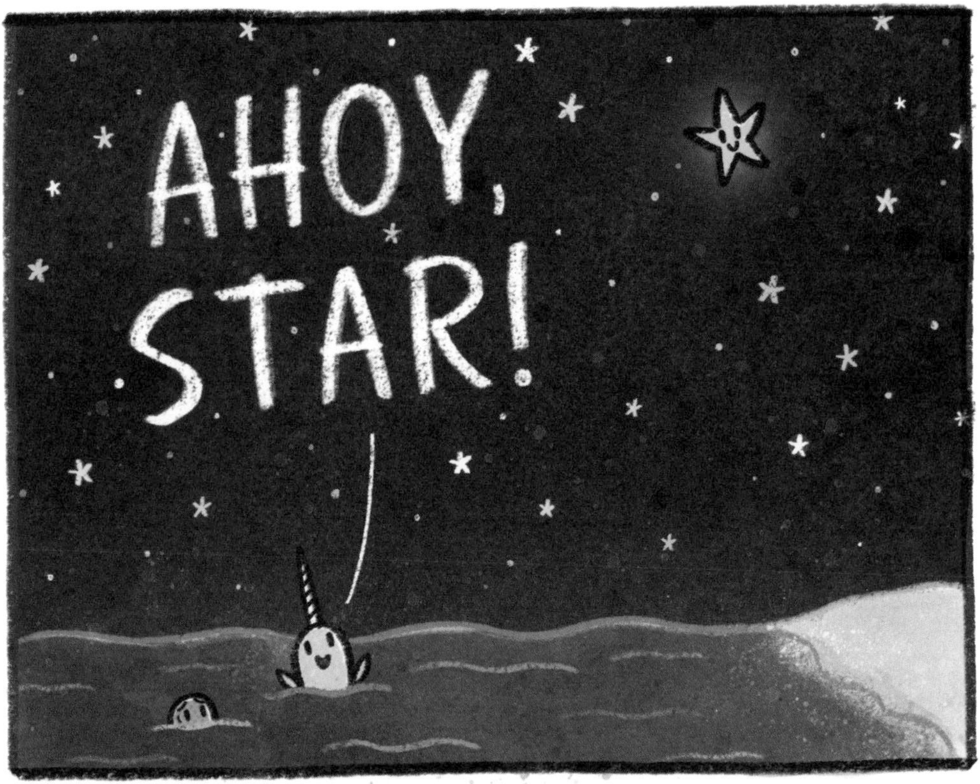
AHOY, STAR!

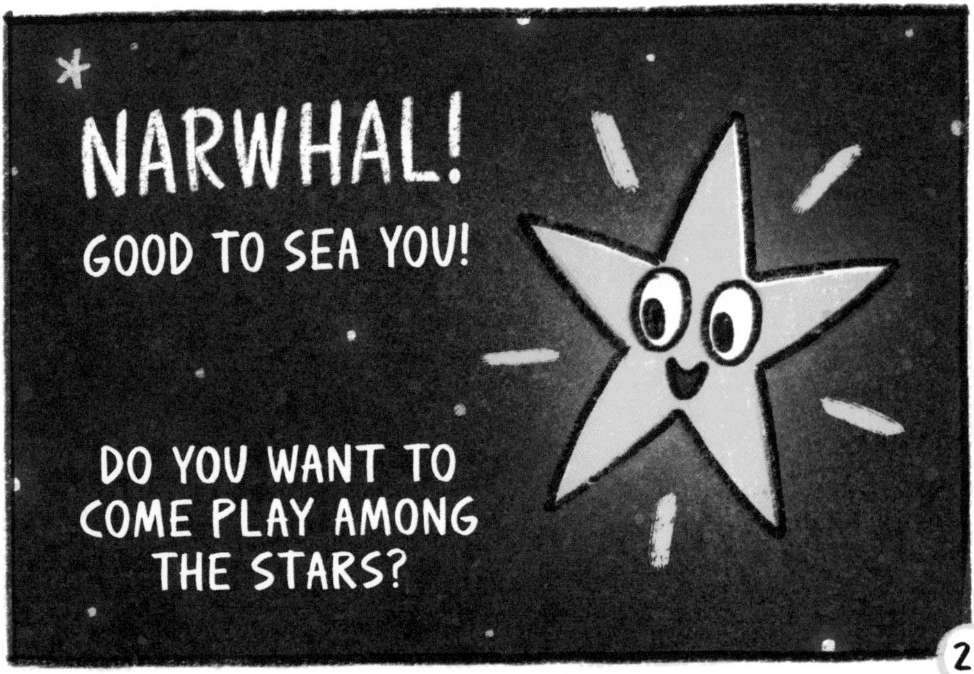
NARWHAL!
GOOD TO SEA YOU!
DO YOU WANT TO COME PLAY AMONG THE STARS?

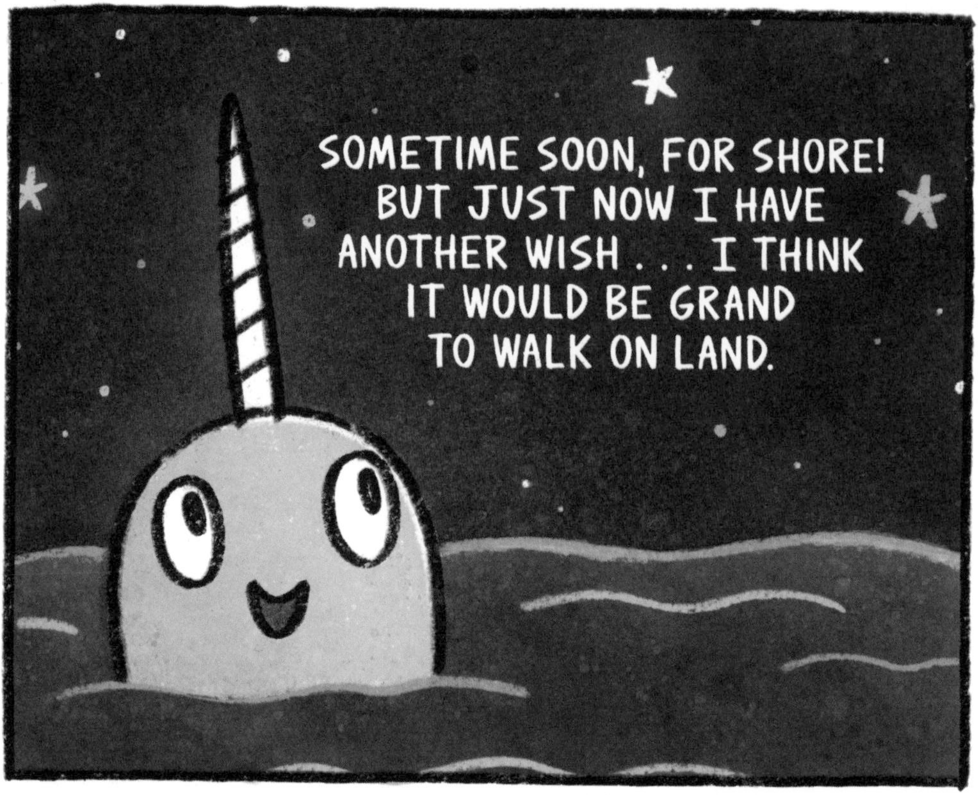
SOMETIME SOON, FOR SHORE! BUT JUST NOW I HAVE ANOTHER WISH . . . I THINK IT WOULD BE GRAND TO WALK ON LAND.

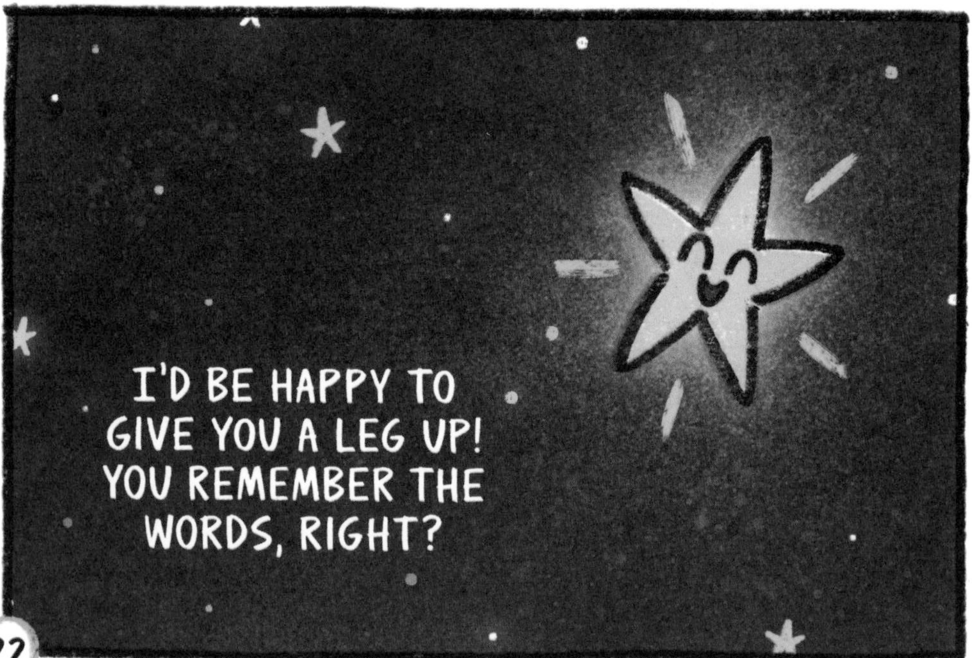
I'D BE HAPPY TO GIVE YOU A LEG UP! YOU REMEMBER THE WORDS, RIGHT?

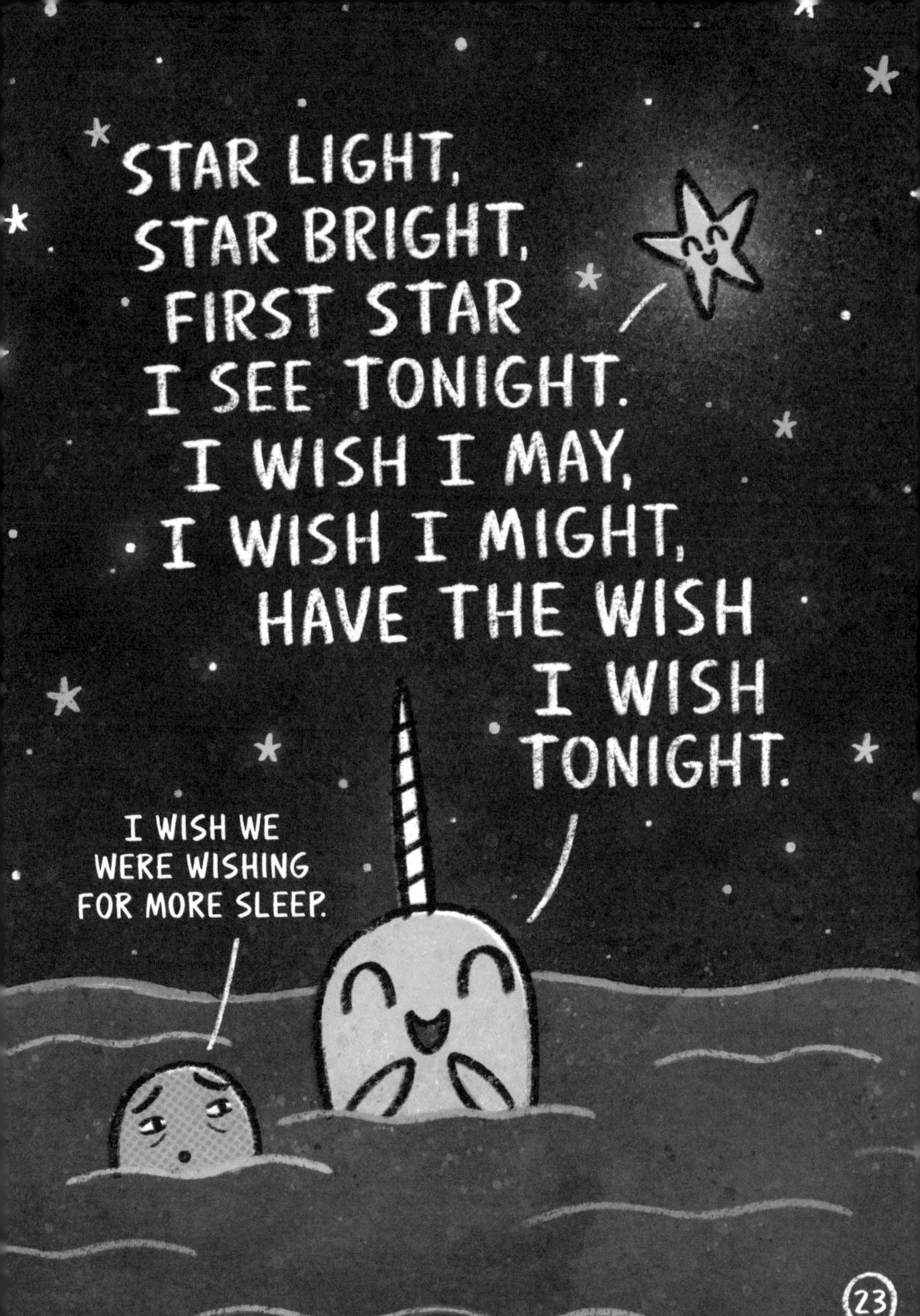
STAR LIGHT, STAR BRIGHT, FIRST STAR I SEE TONIGHT. I WISH I MAY, I WISH I MIGHT, HAVE THE WISH I WISH TONIGHT.
I WISH WE WERE WISHING FOR MORE SLEEP.

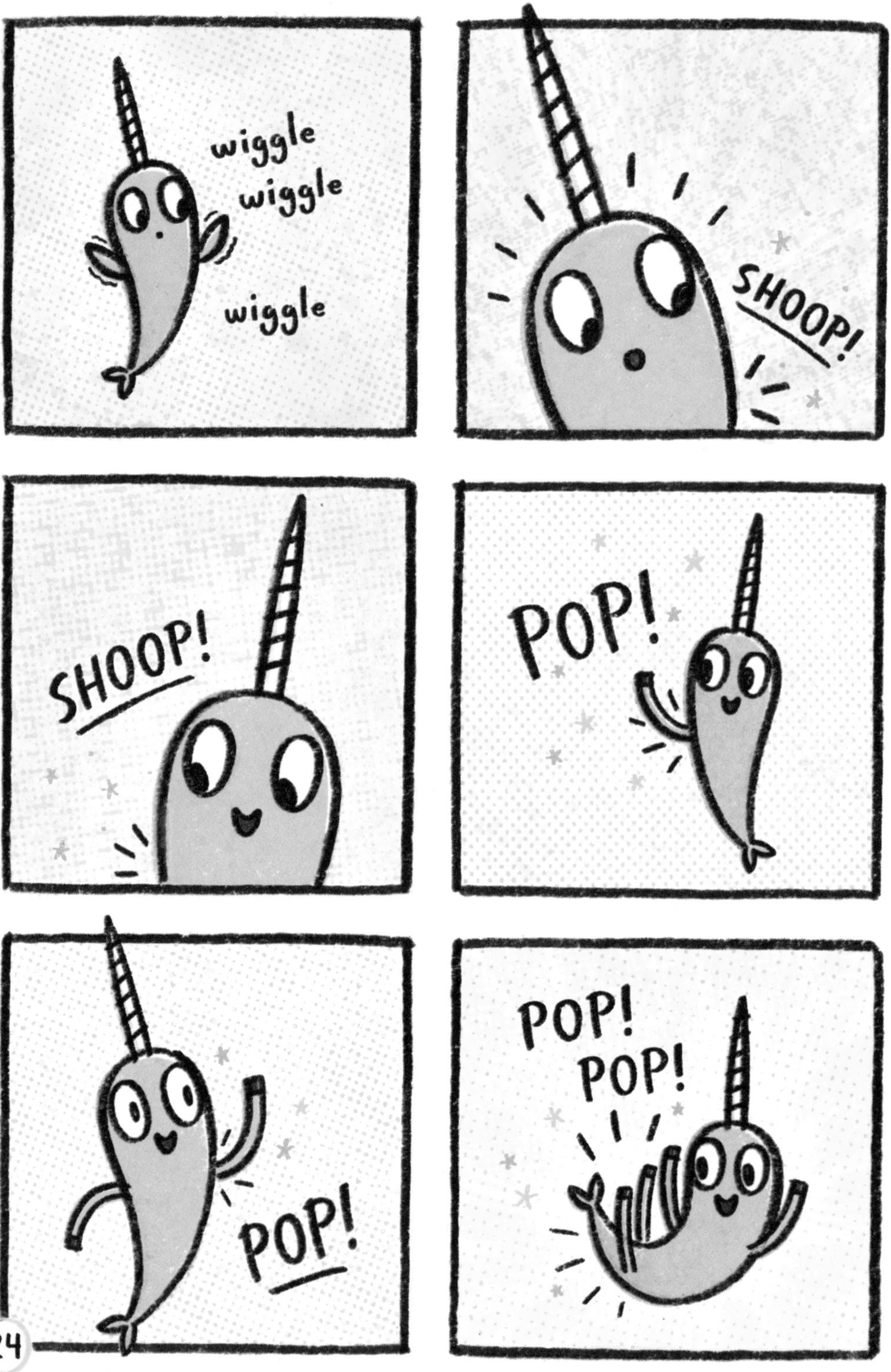
wiggle
wiggle
wiggle
SHOOP!
SHOOP!
POP!
POP!
POP!
POP!

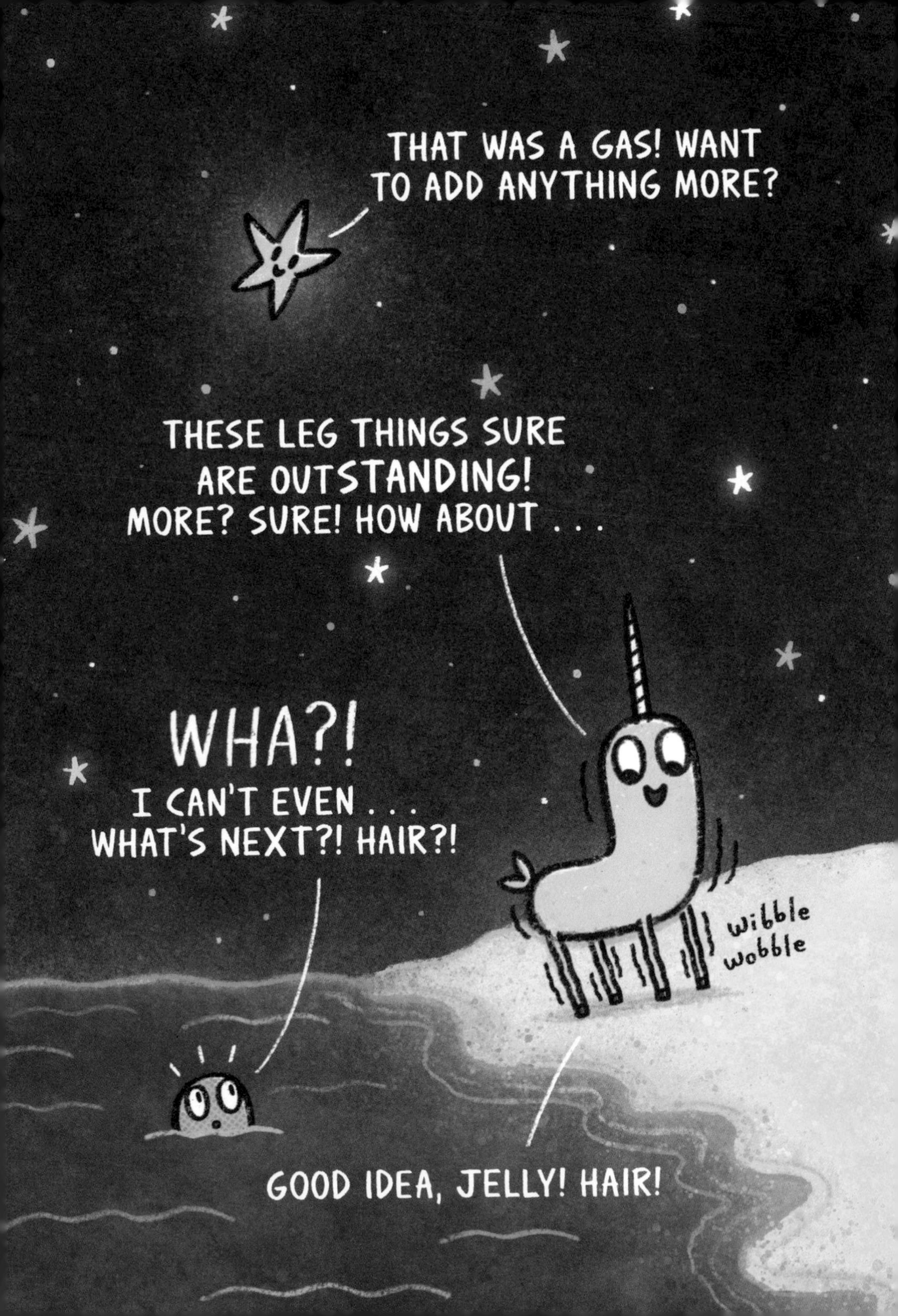
THAT WAS A GAS! WANT TO ADD ANYTHING MORE?
THESE LEG THINGS SURE ARE OUTSTANDING! MORE? SURE! HOW ABOUT . . .
WHA?! I CAN'T EVEN . . . WHAT'S NEXT?! HAIR?!
wibble wobble
GOOD IDEA, JELLY! HAIR!

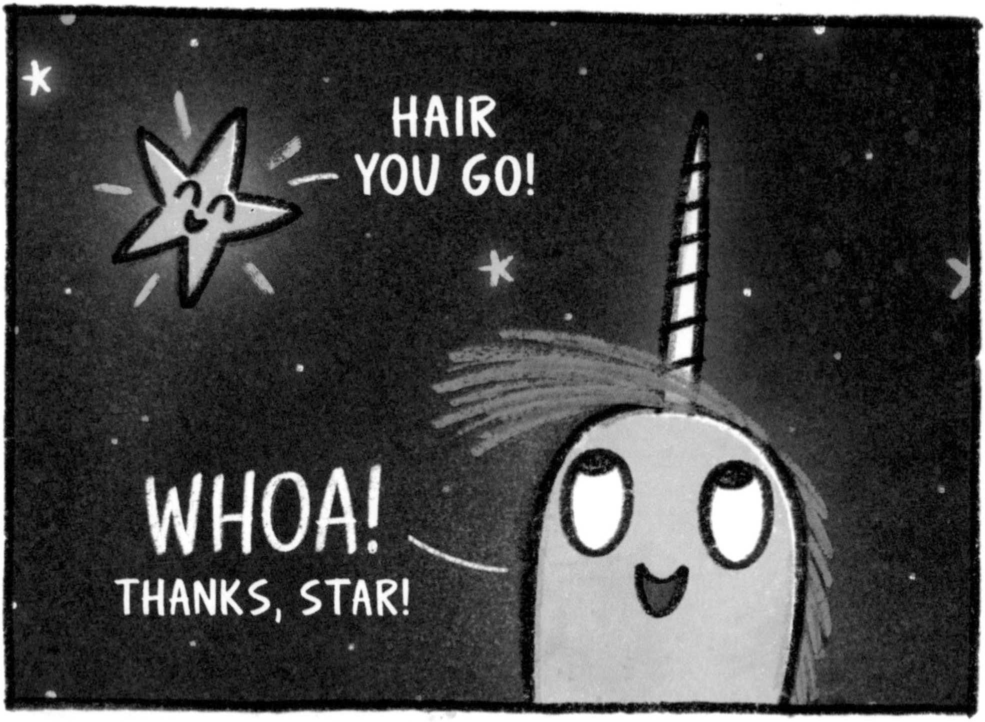
HAIR YOU GO!
WHOA! THANKS, STAR!

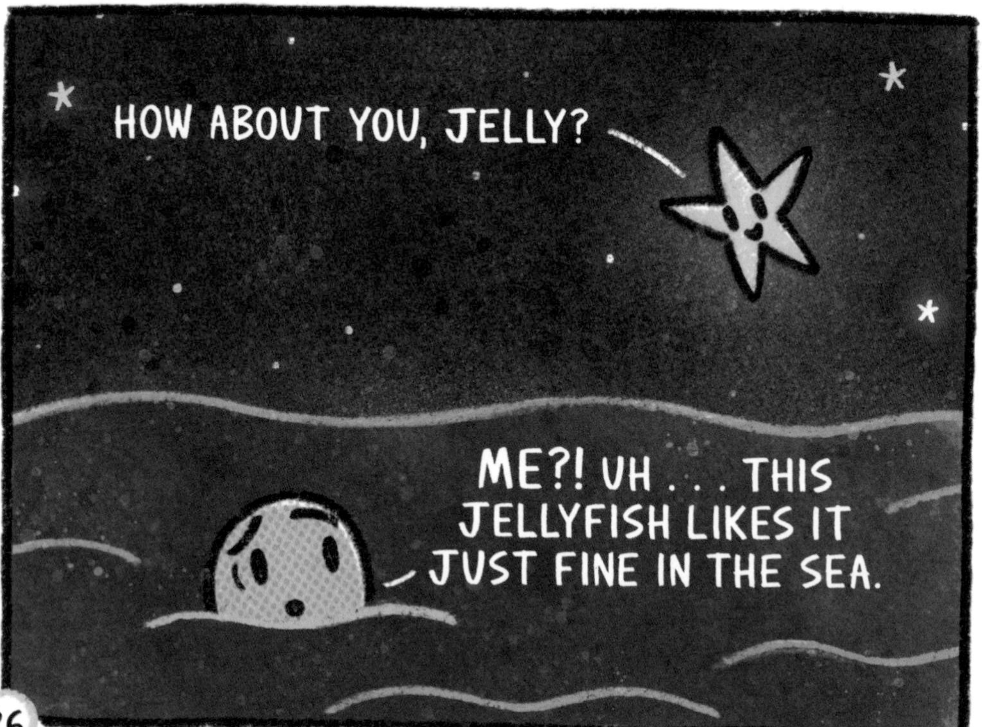
HOW ABOUT YOU, JELLY?
ME?! UH . . . THIS JELLYFISH LIKES IT JUST FINE IN THE SEA.

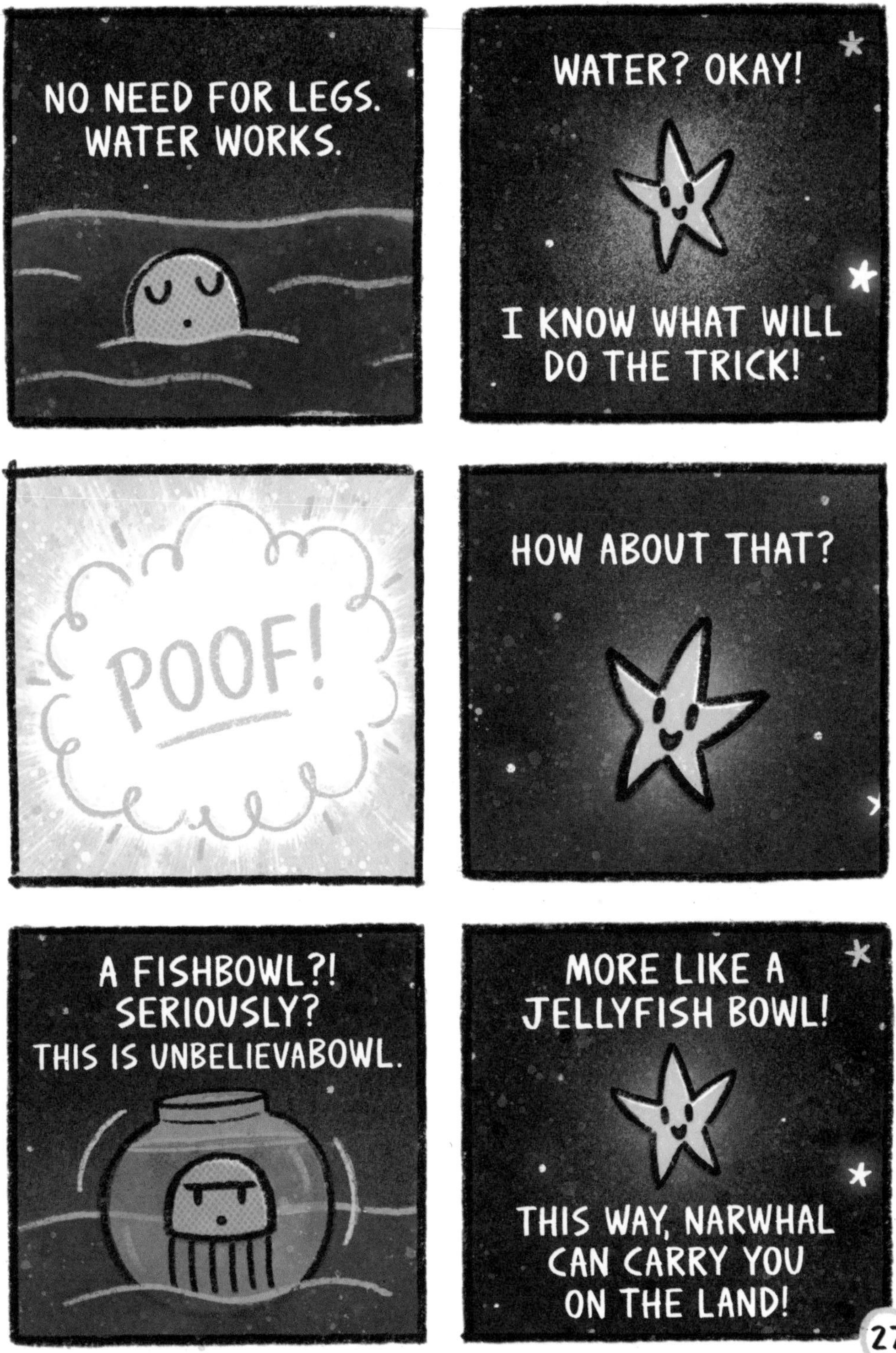
NO NEED FOR LEGS. WATER WORKS.
WATER? OKAY!
I KNOW WHAT WILL DO THE TRICK!
POOF!
HOW ABOUT THAT?
A FISHBOWL?! SERIOUSLY? THIS IS UNBELIEVABOWL.
MORE LIKE A JELLYFISH BOWL!
THIS WAY, NARWHAL CAN CARRY YOU ON THE LAND!

WELL, THAT'S JUST . . . GRAND.

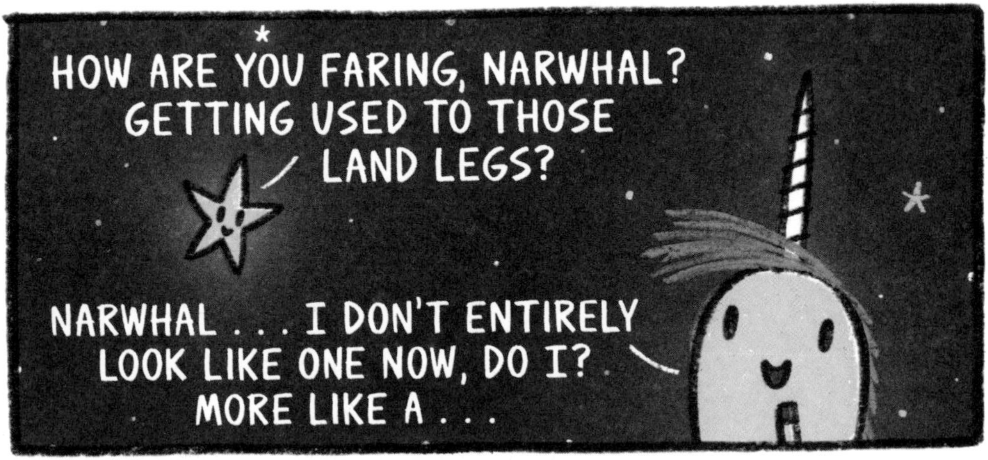
HOW ARE YOU FARING, NARWHAL? GETTING USED TO THOSE LAND LEGS?
NARWHAL . . . I DON'T ENTIRELY LOOK LIKE ONE NOW, DO I? MORE LIKE A . . .

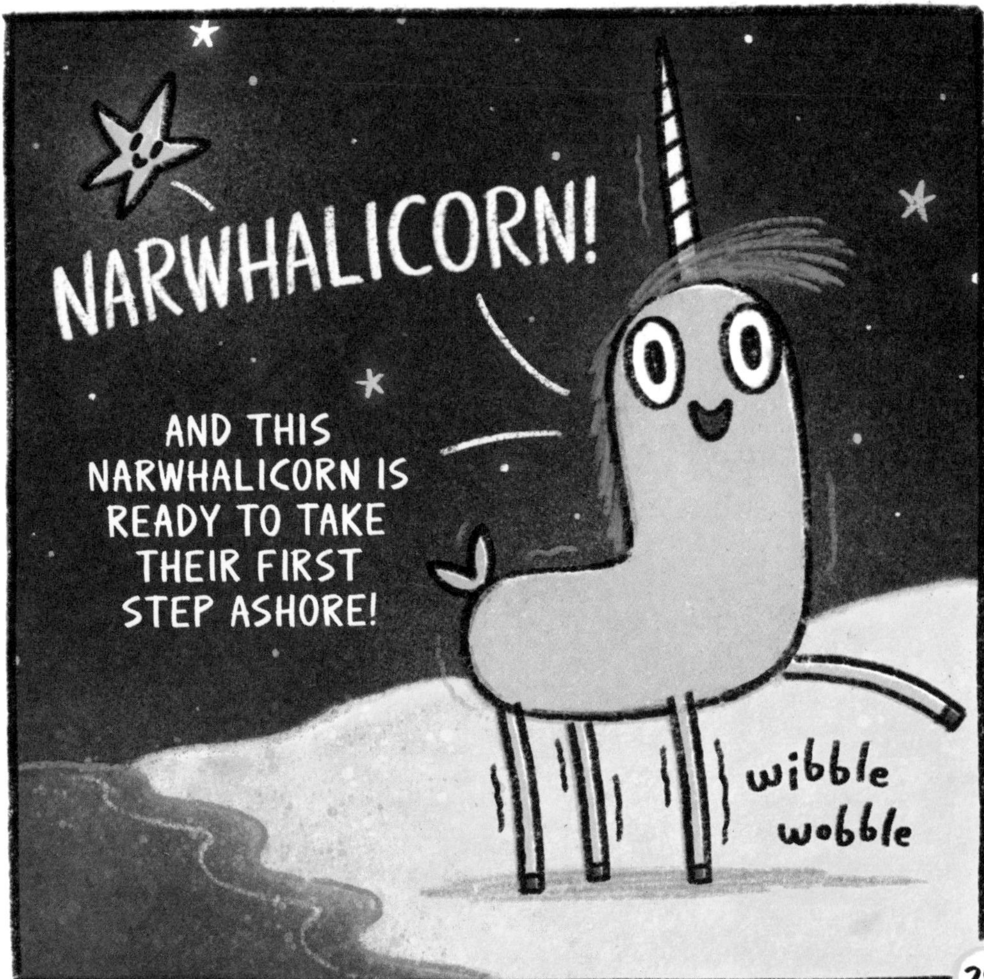
NARWHALICORN!
AND THIS NARWHALICORN IS READY TO TAKE THEIR FIRST STEP ASHORE!
wibble wobble

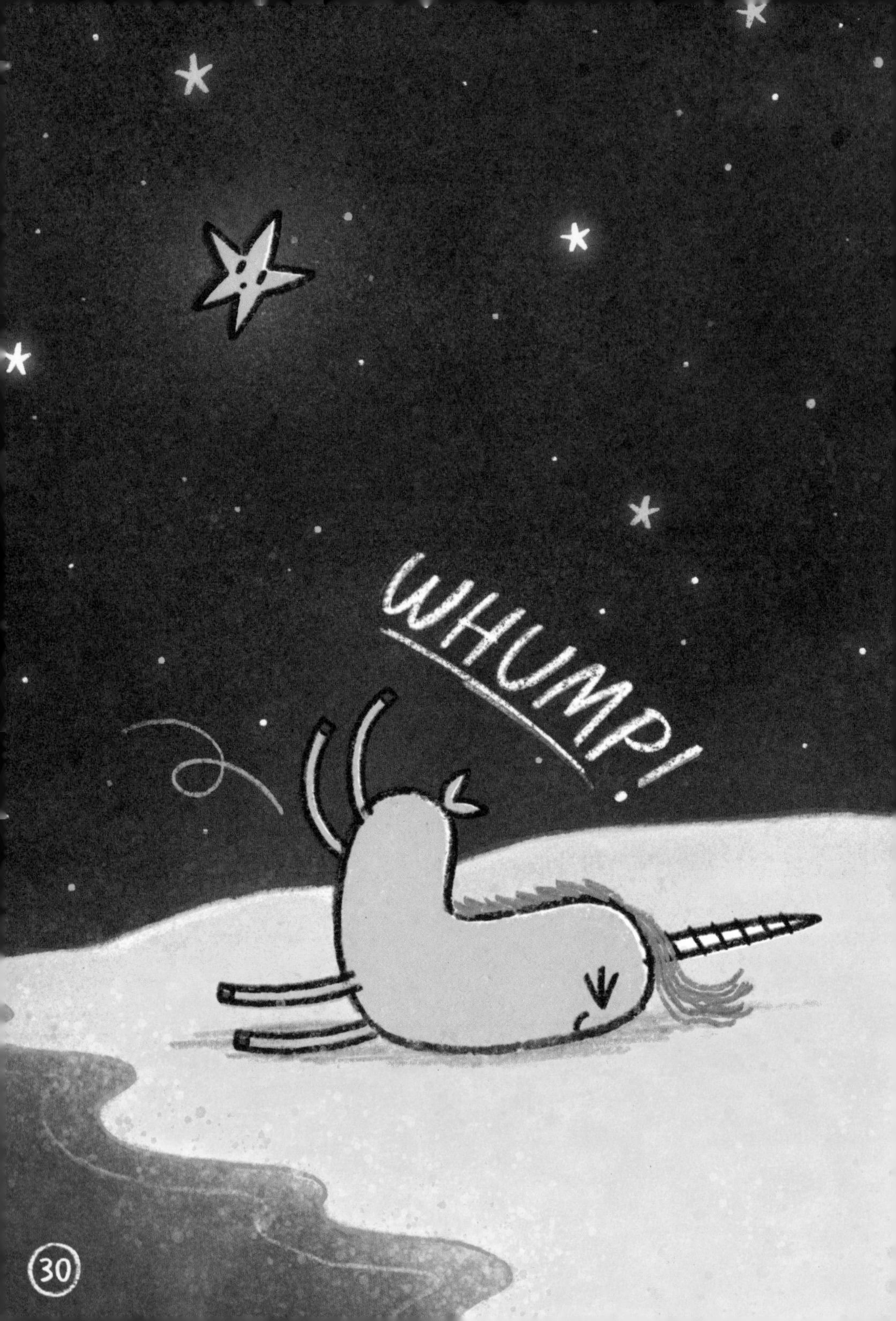
WHUMP!

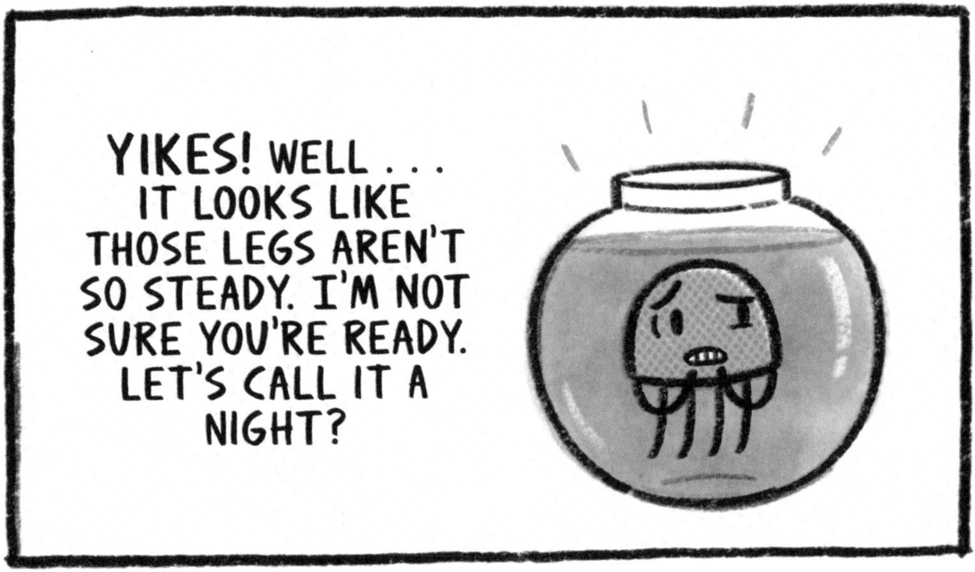
YIKES! WELL . . . IT LOOKS LIKE THOSE LEGS AREN'T SO STEADY. I'M NOT SURE YOU'RE READY. LET'S CALL IT A NIGHT?

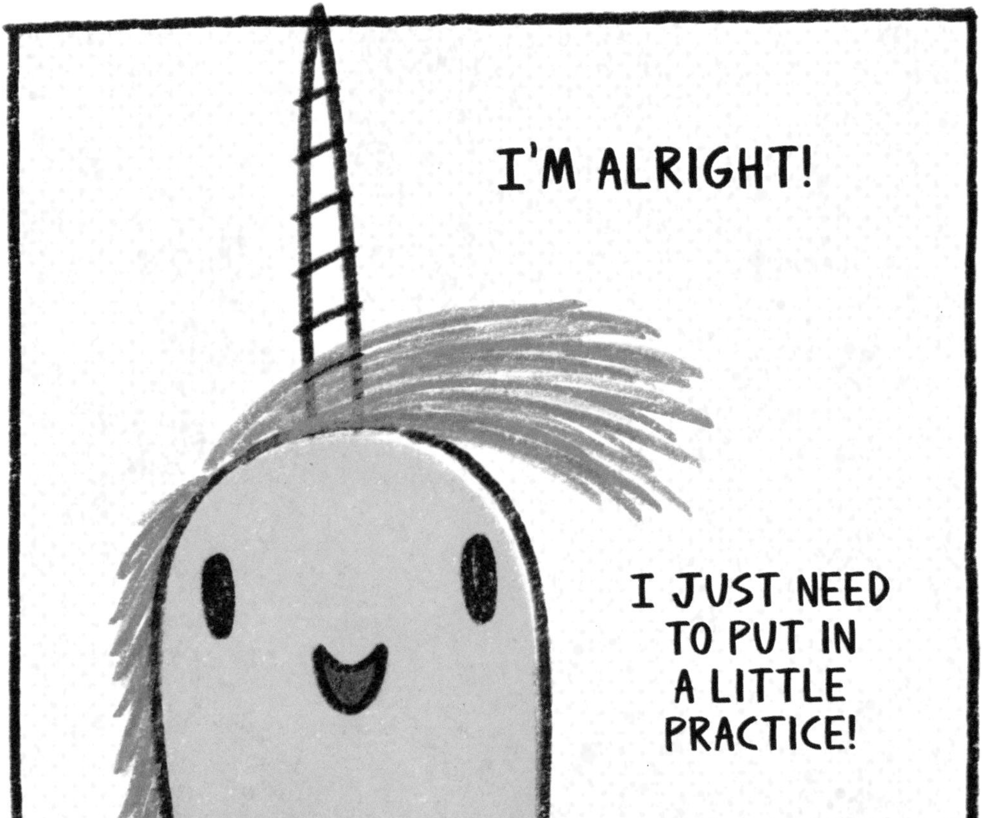
I'M ALRIGHT!
I JUST NEED TO PUT IN A LITTLE PRACTICE!

ELEVEN MINUTES LATER . . .

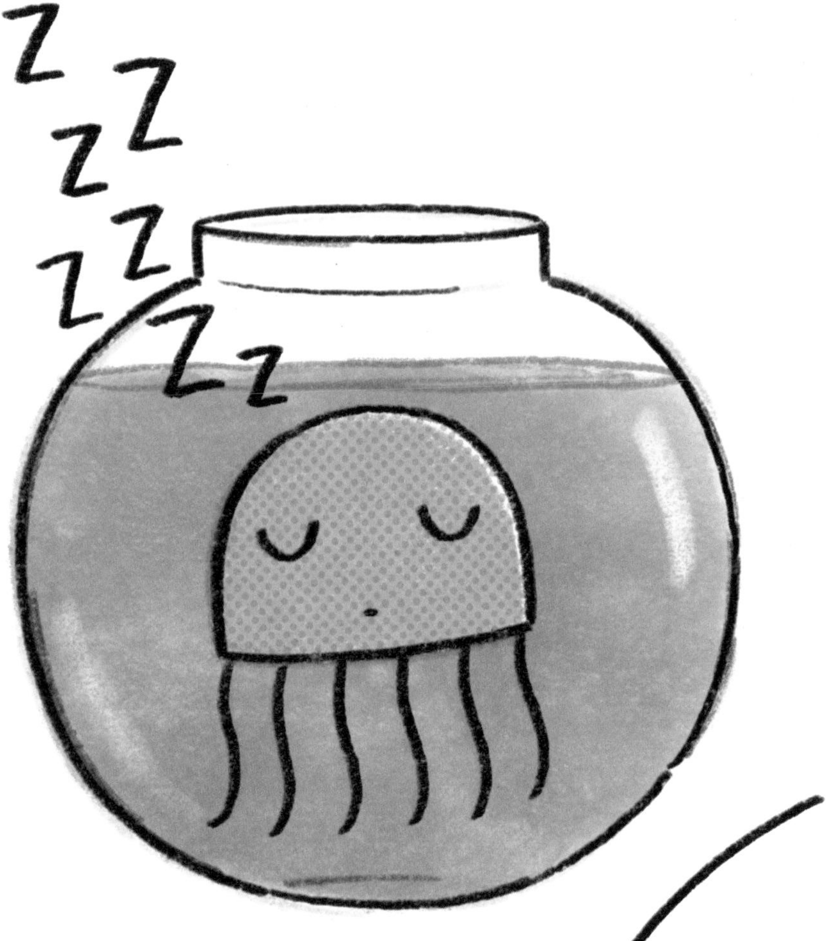

I'VE GOT IT!

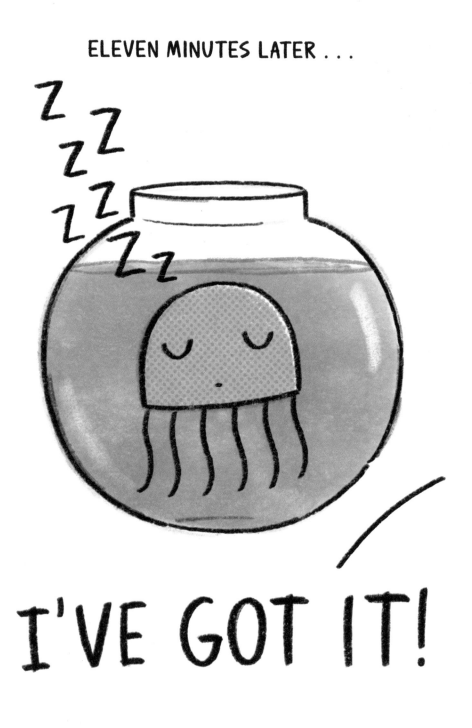

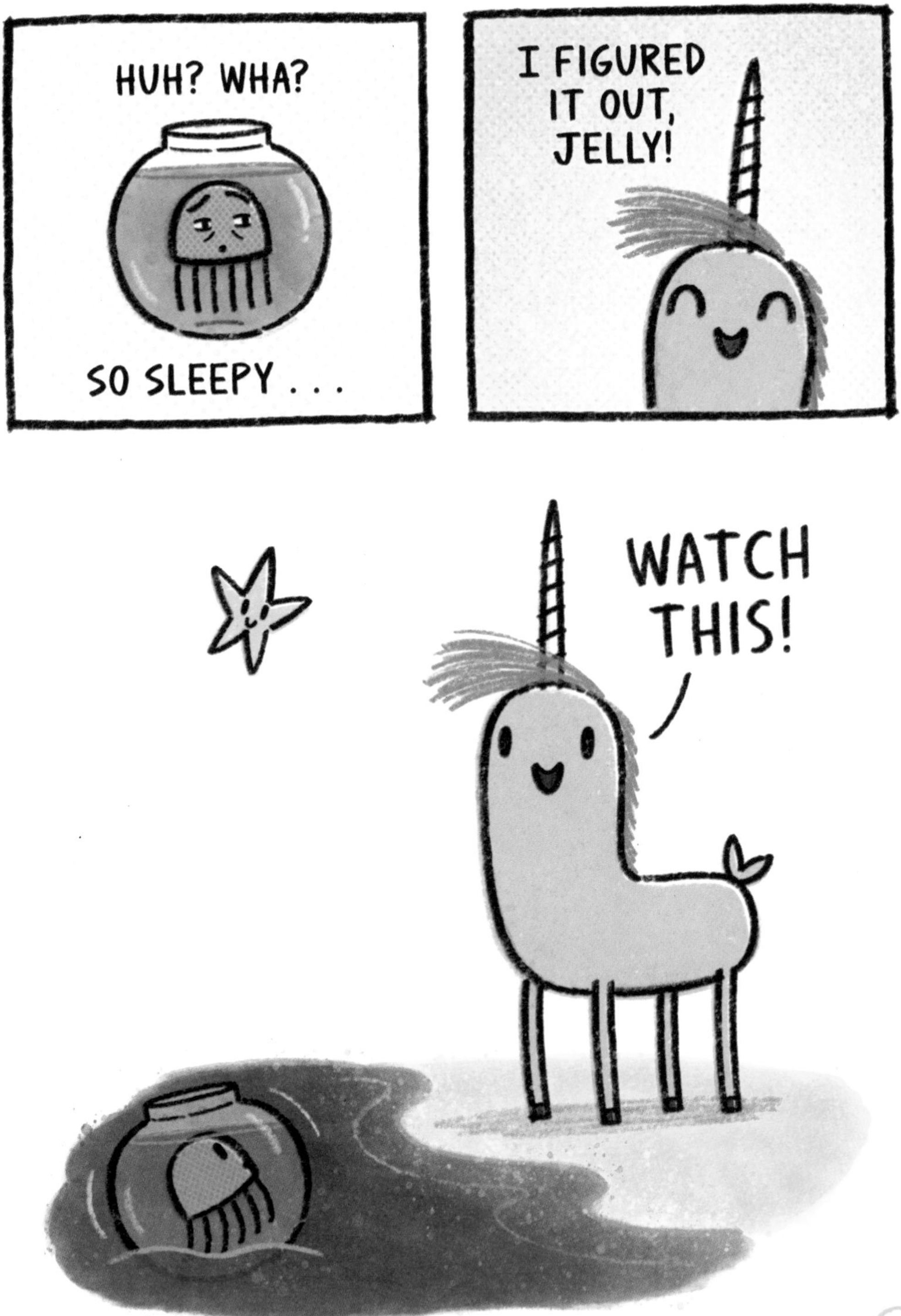
HUH? WHA?
SO SLEEPY . . .
I FIGURED IT OUT, JELLY!
WATCH THIS!

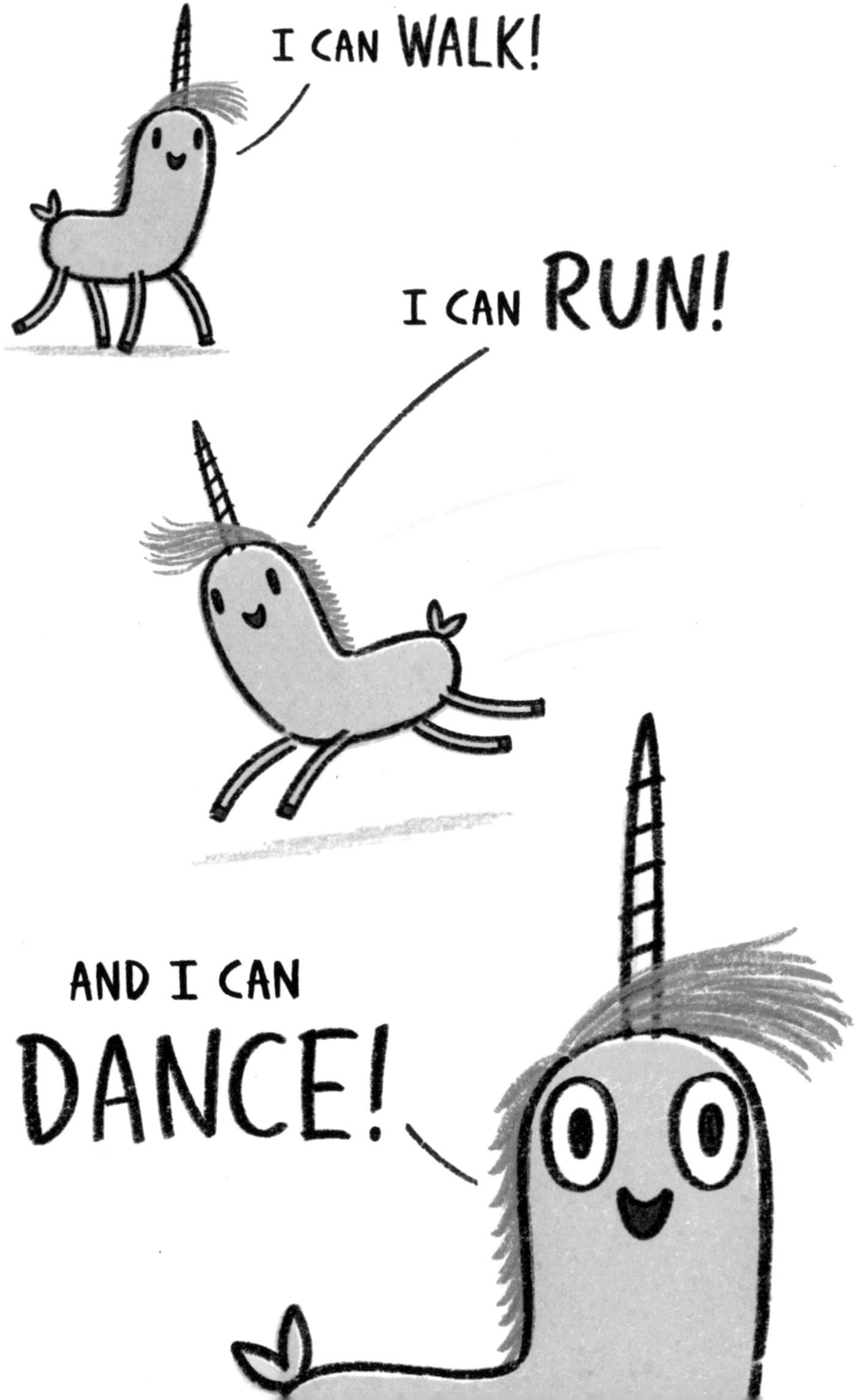
I CAN WALK!
I CAN RUN!
AND I CAN DANCE!

THE NARWHALICORN DANCE

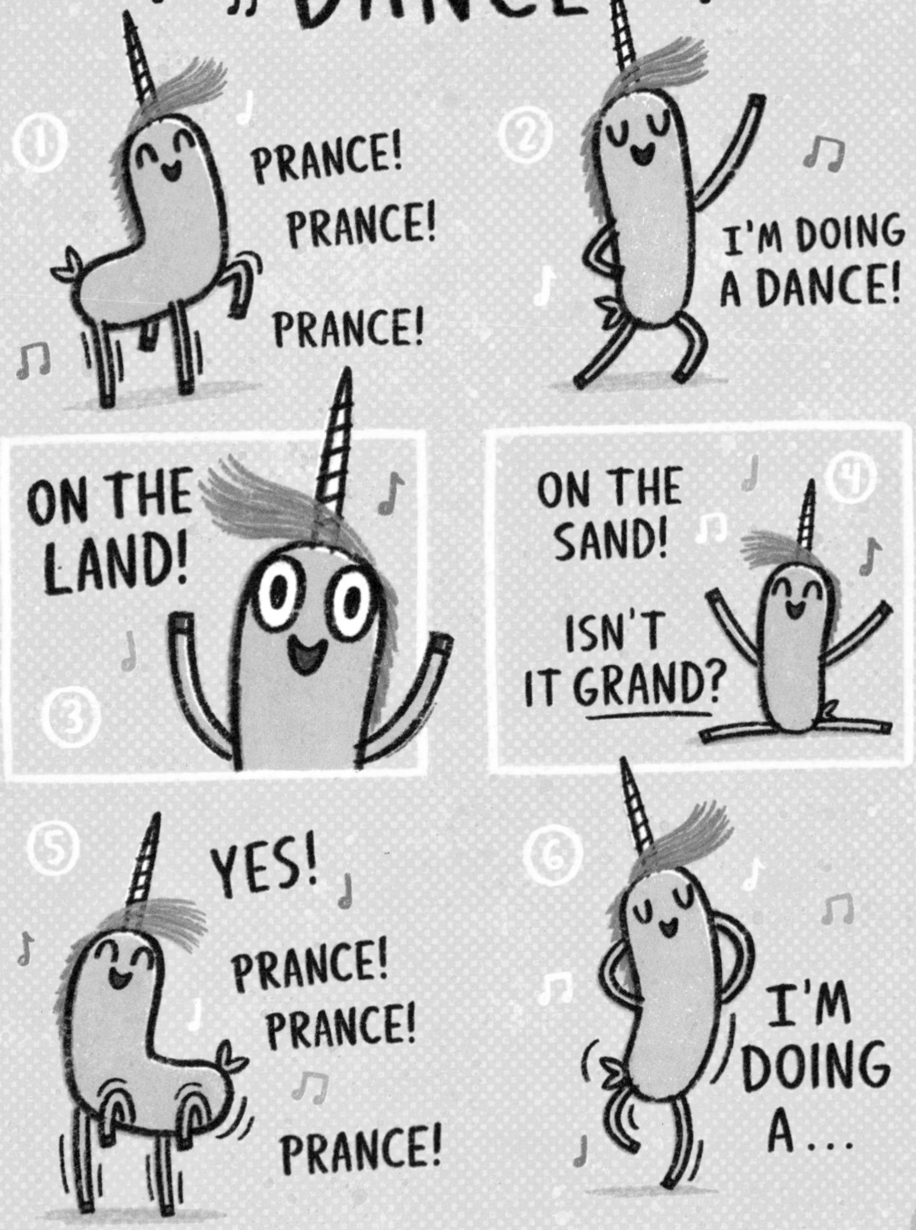

1
PRANCE!
PRANCE!
PRANCE!
2
I'M DOING A DANCE!
ON THE LAND!
3
ON THE SAND!
ISN'T IT GRAND?
4
5
YES!
PRANCE!
PRANCE!
PRANCE!
6
I'M DOING A...

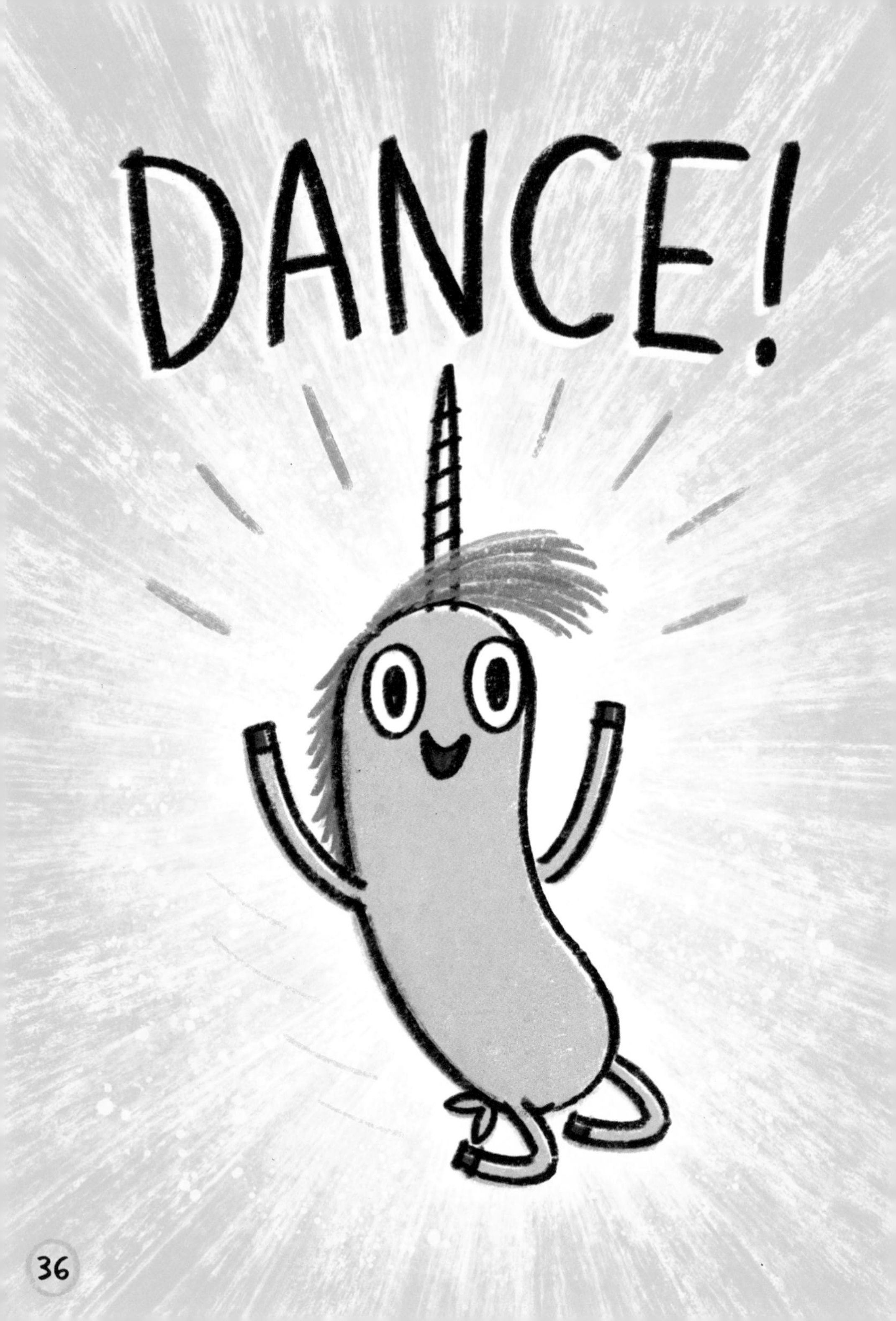
DANCE!

NARWHALICORN
IS
OUT-OF-THIS-
WORLD!

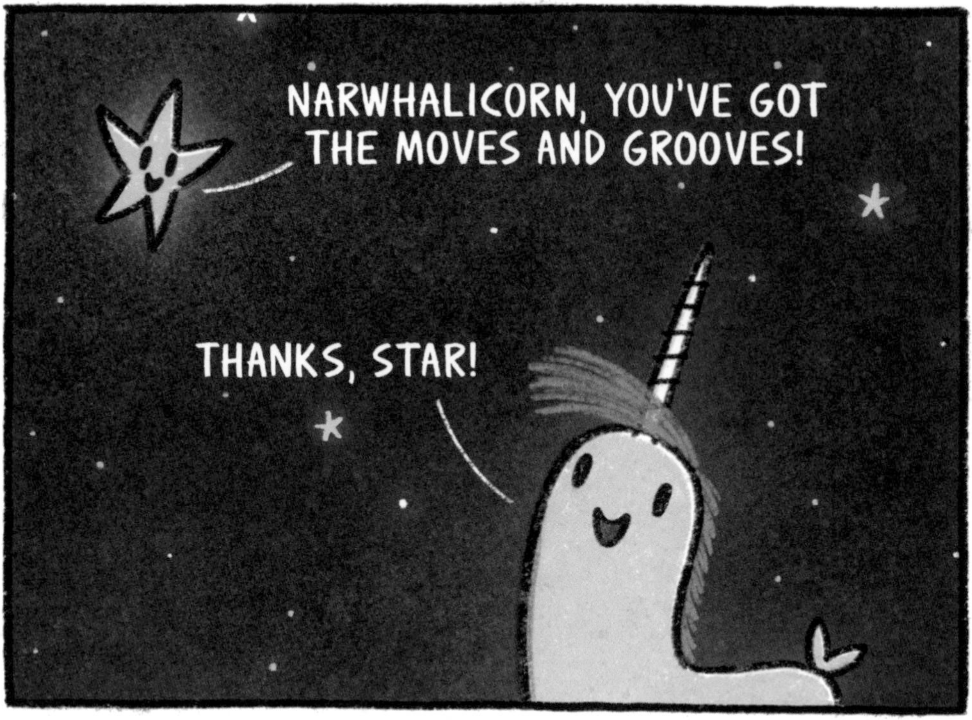
NARWHALICORN, YOU'VE GOT THE MOVES AND GROOVES!
THANKS, STAR!

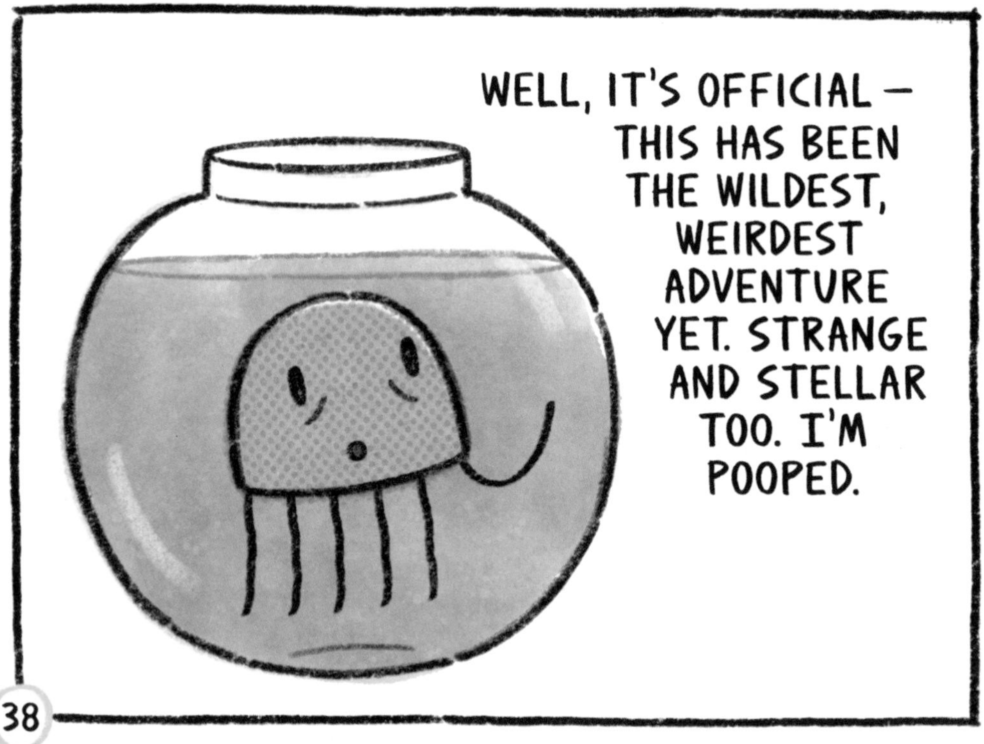
WELL, IT'S OFFICIAL — THIS HAS BEEN THE WILDEST, WEIRDEST ADVENTURE YET. STRANGE AND STELLAR TOO. I'M POOPED.

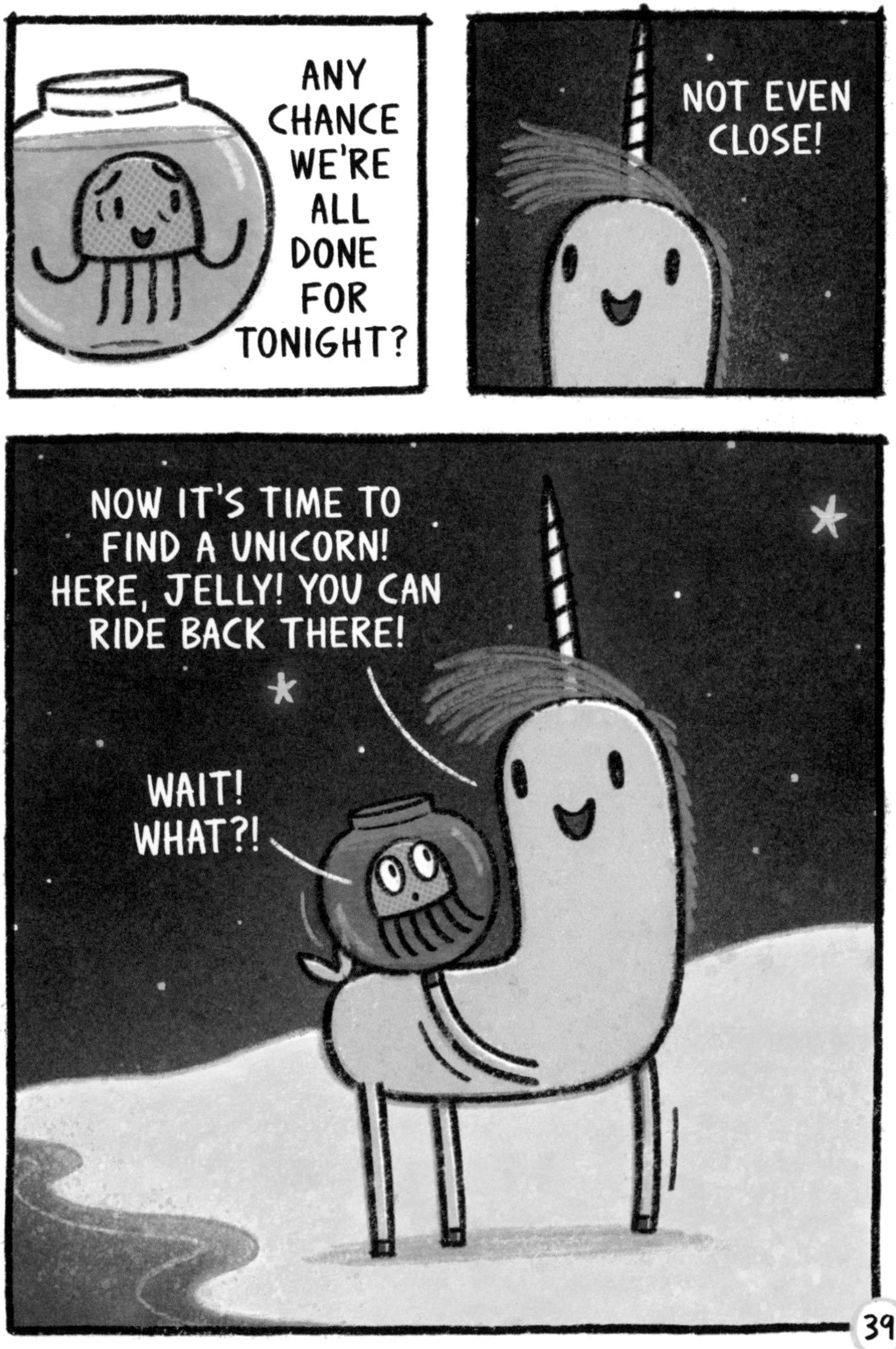
ANY CHANCE WE'RE ALL DONE FOR TONIGHT?
NOT EVEN CLOSE!
NOW IT'S TIME TO FIND A UNICORN! HERE, JELLY! YOU CAN RIDE BACK THERE!
WAIT! WHAT?!

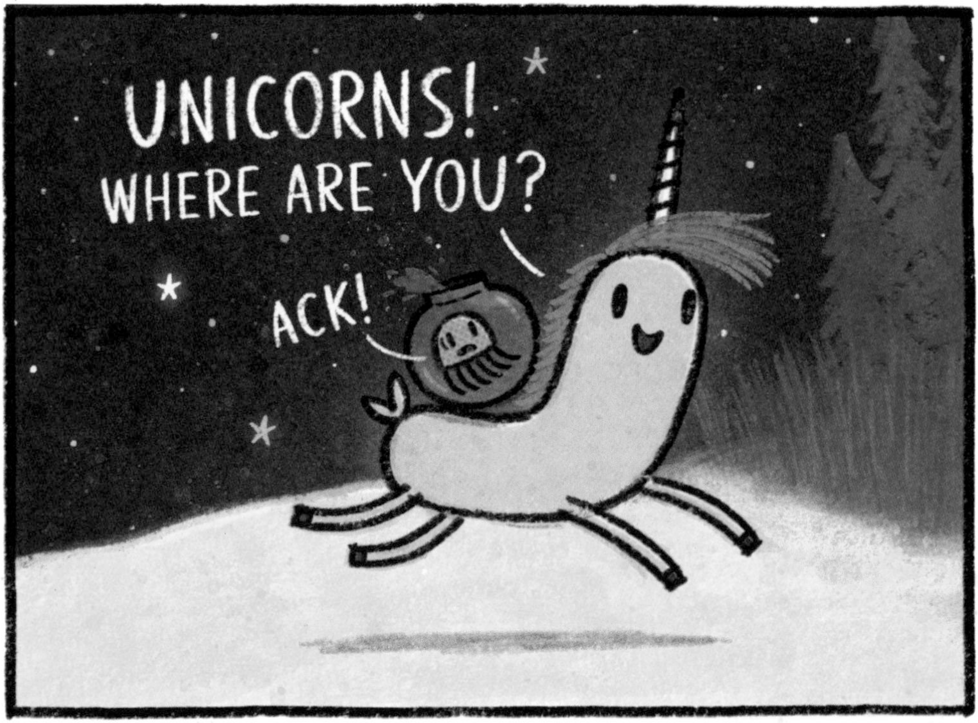
UNICORNS! WHERE ARE YOU?
ACK!

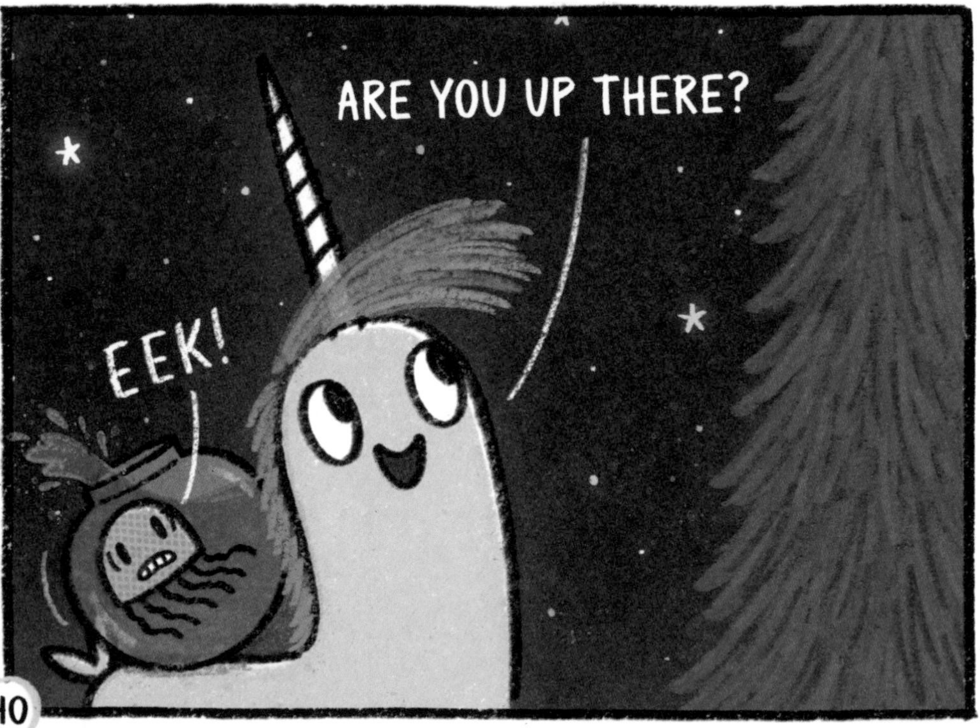
ARE YOU UP THERE?
EEK!

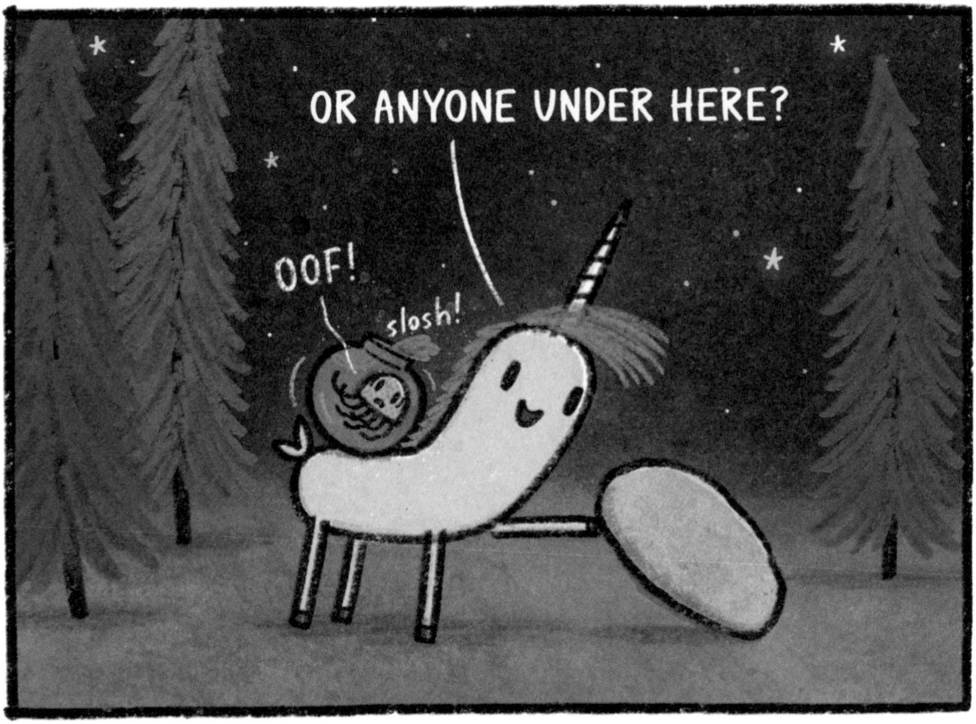
OR ANYONE UNDER HERE?
OOF!
slosh!

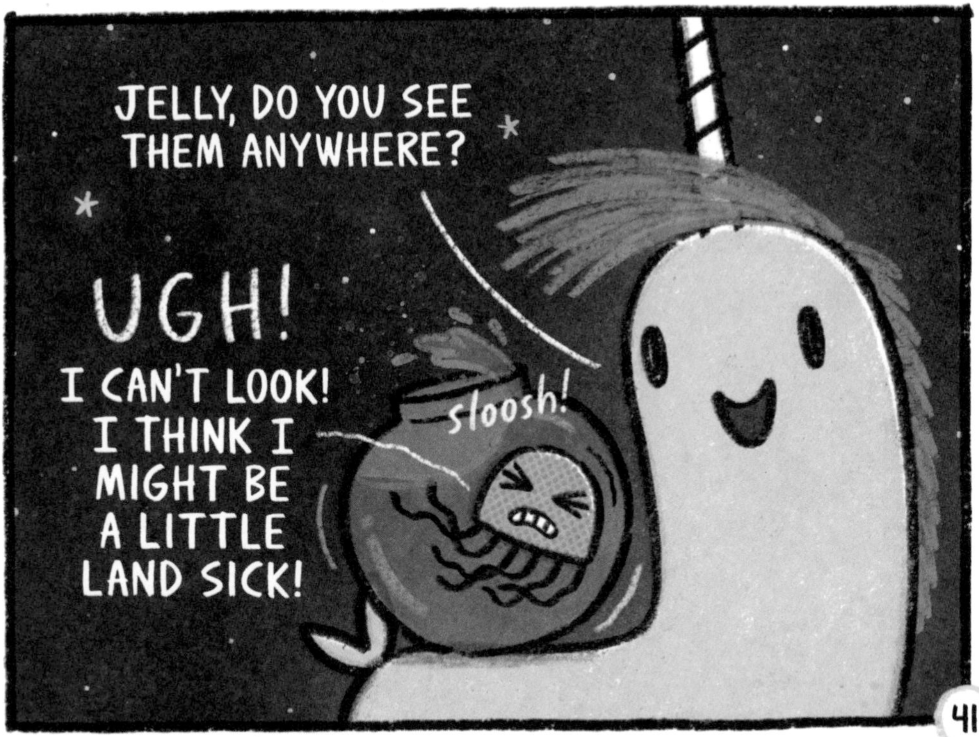
JELLY, DO YOU SEE THEM ANYWHERE?
UGH!
I CAN'T LOOK! I THINK I MIGHT BE A LITTLE LAND SICK!
sloosh!

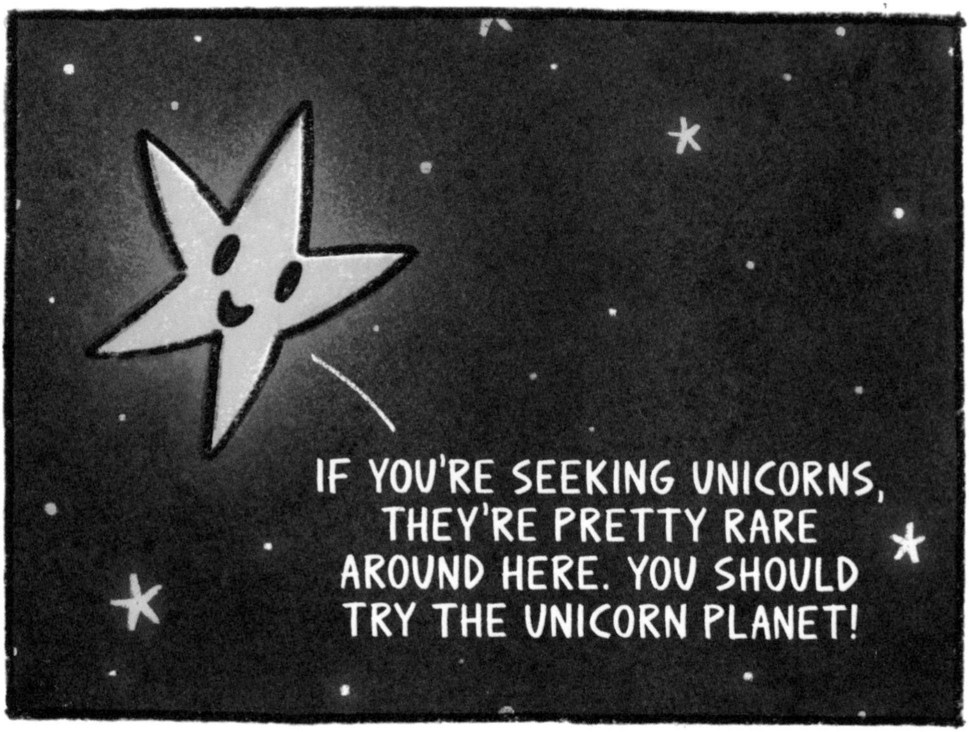
IF YOU'RE SEEKING UNICORNS, THEY'RE PRETTY RARE AROUND HERE. YOU SHOULD TRY THE UNICORN PLANET!

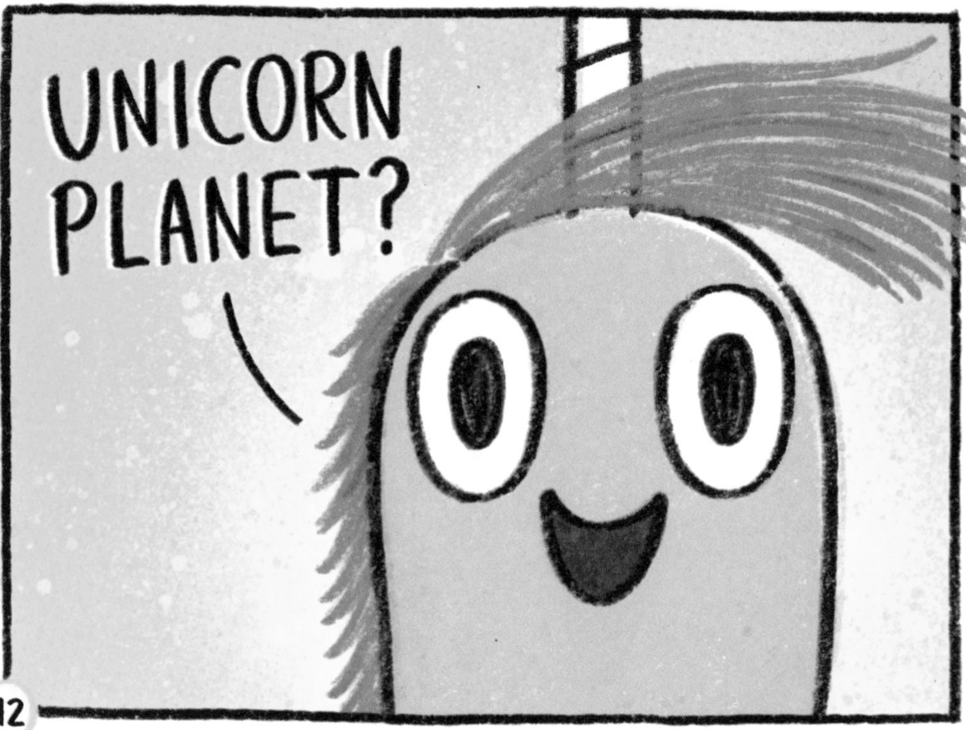
UNICORN PLANET?

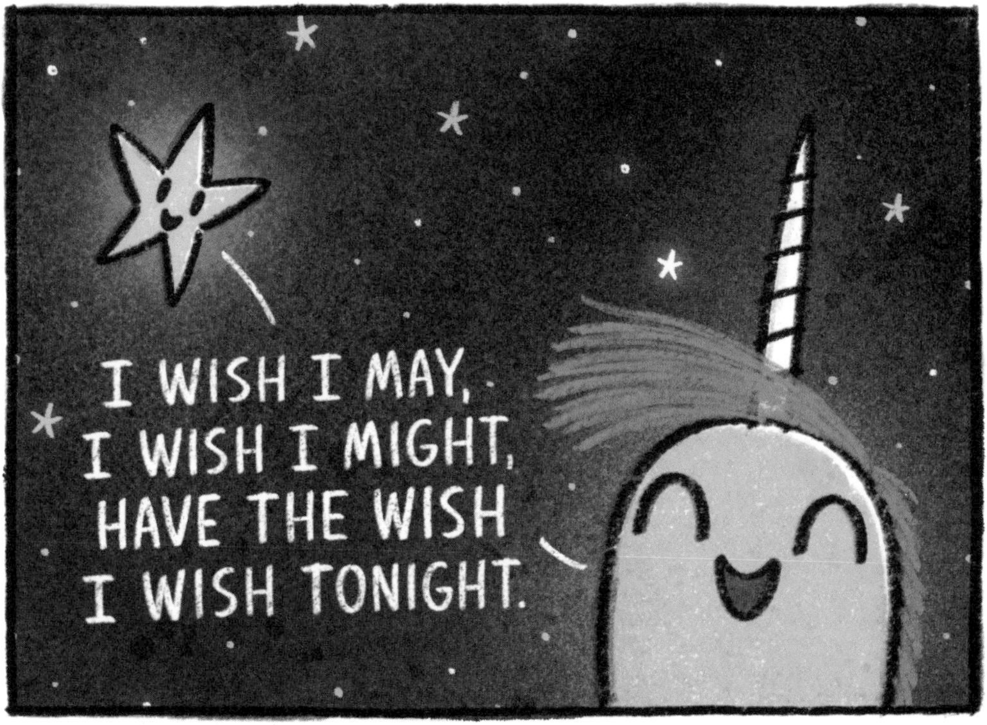
I WISH I MAY,
I WISH I MIGHT,
HAVE THE WISH
I WISH TONIGHT.

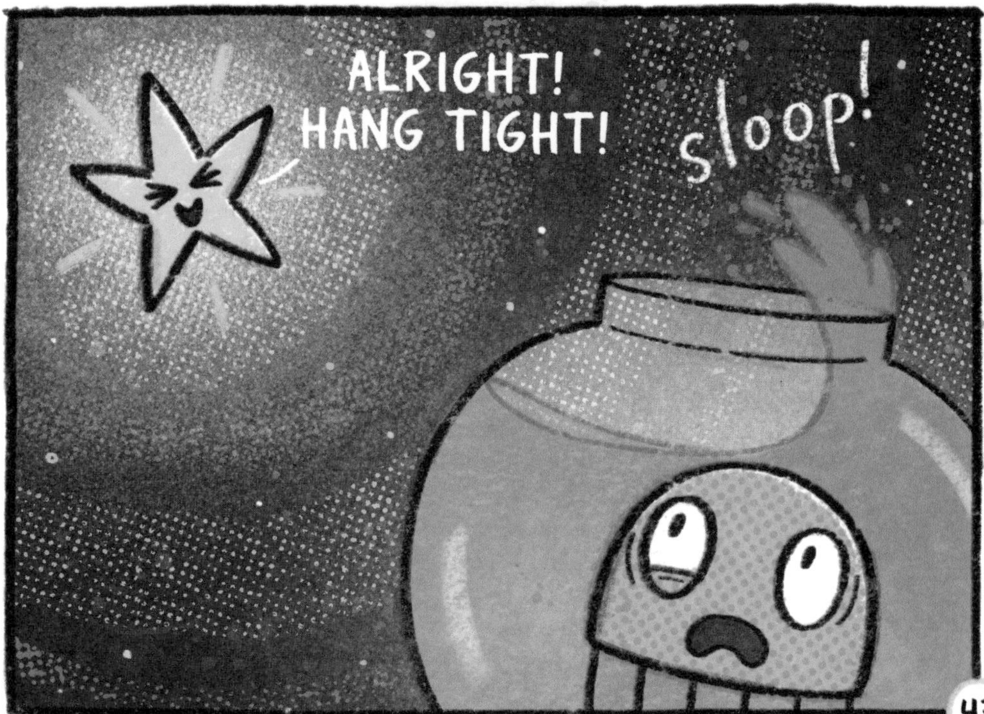
ALRIGHT!
HANG TIGHT!
sloop!

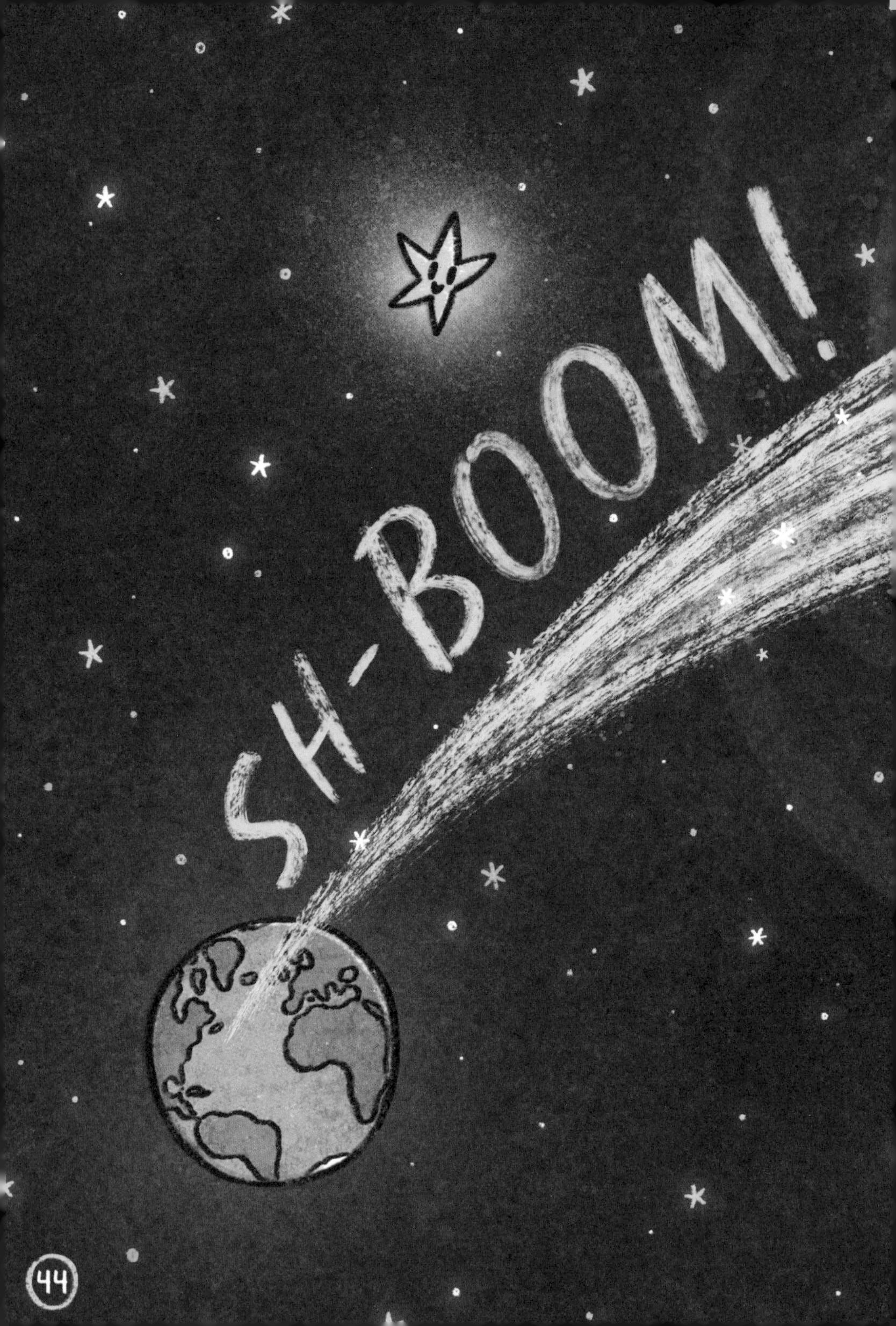
SH-BOOM!

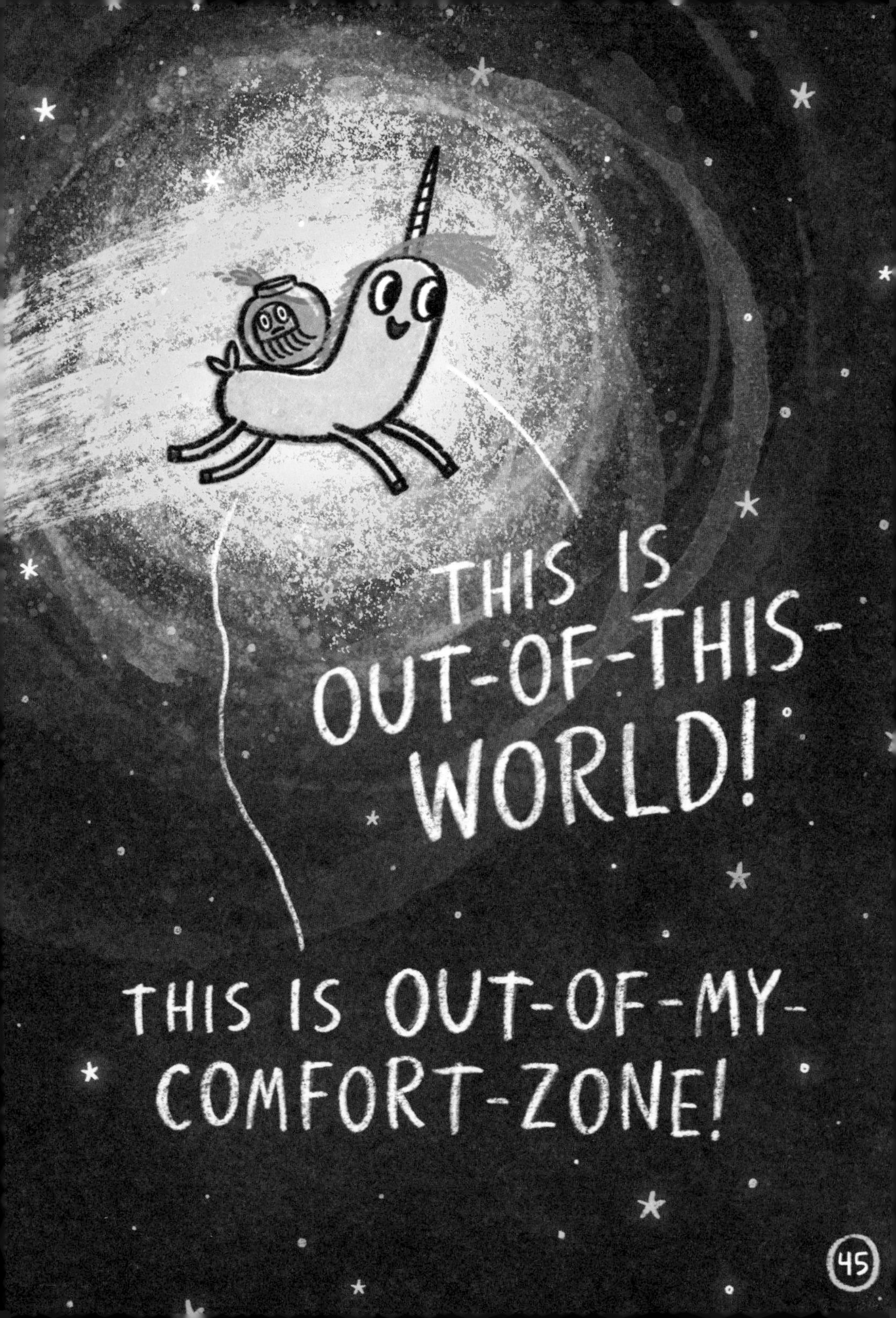
THIS IS OUT-OF-THIS-WORLD!
THIS IS OUT-OF-MY-COMFORT-ZONE!

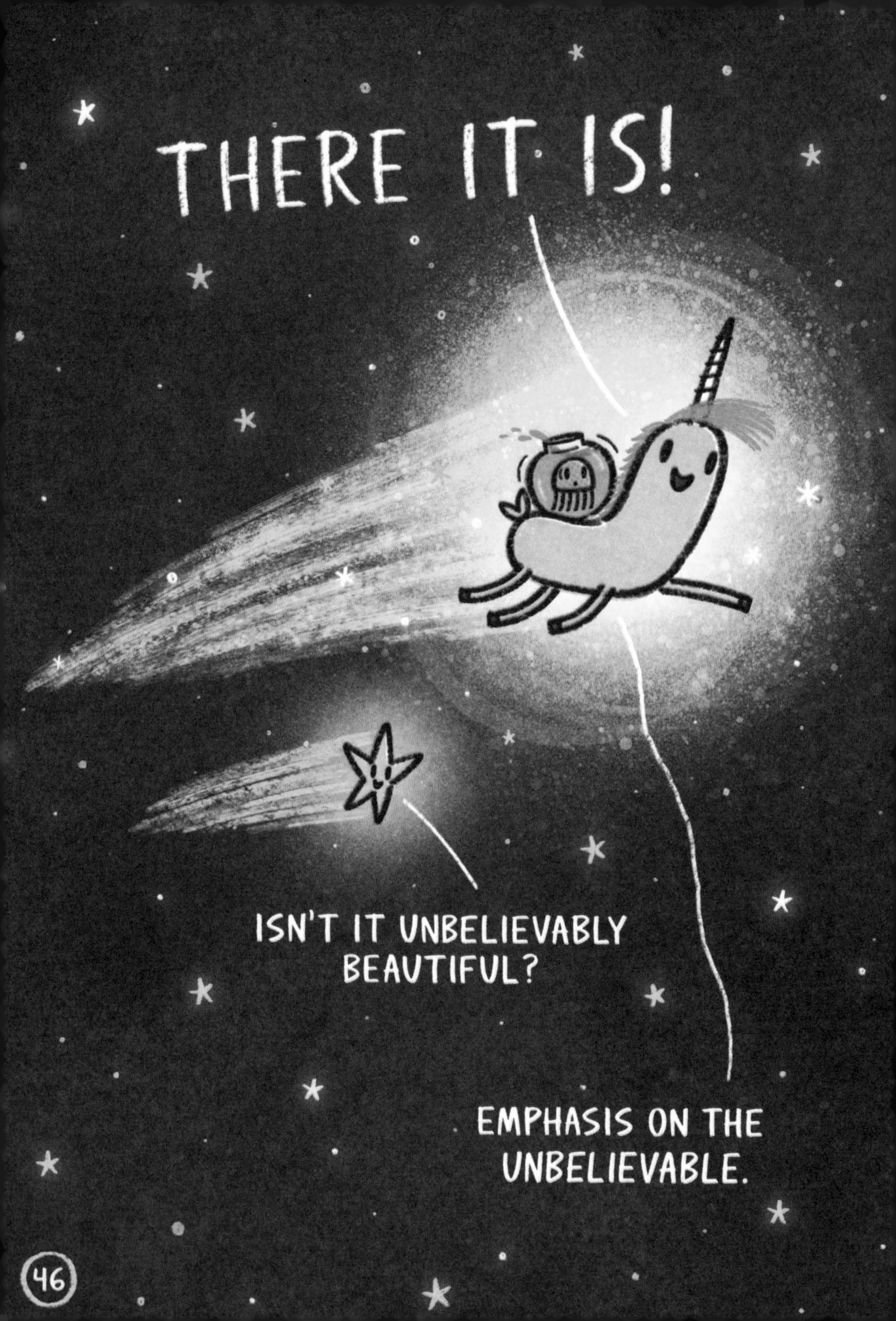
THERE IT IS!
ISN'T IT UNBELIEVABLY BEAUTIFUL?
EMPHASIS ON THE UNBELIEVABLE.

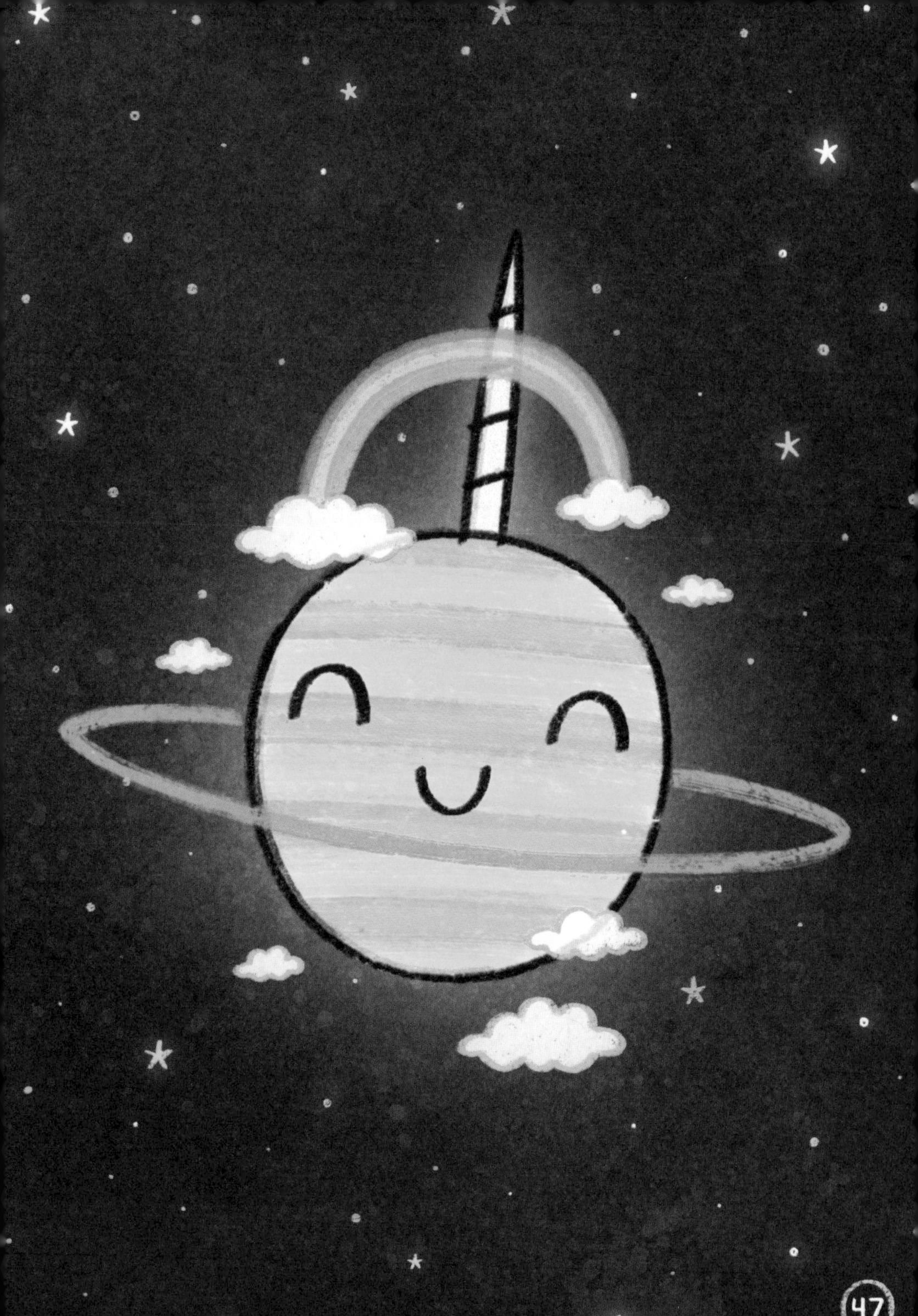

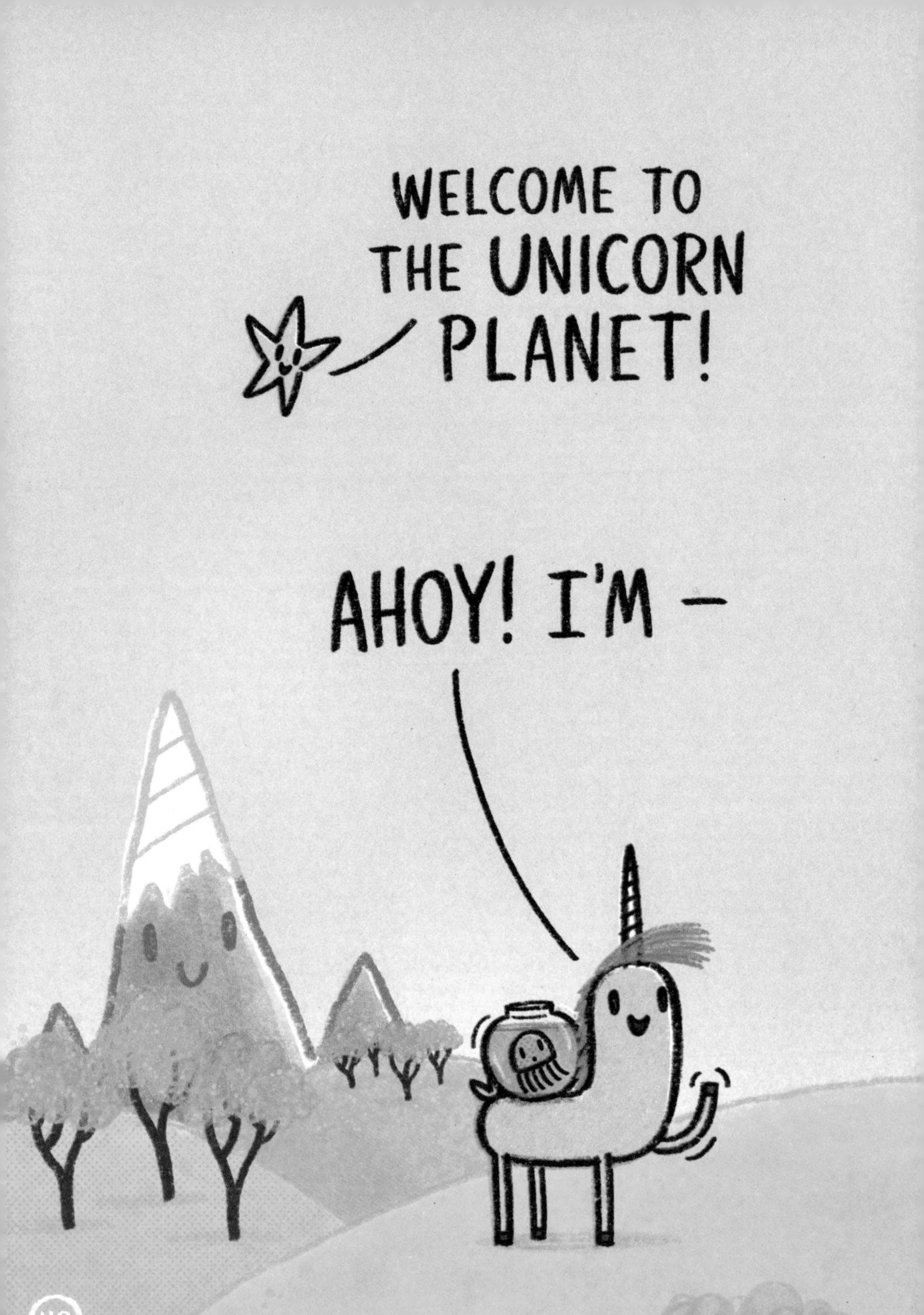
WELCOME TO THE UNICORN PLANET!
AHOY! I'M –

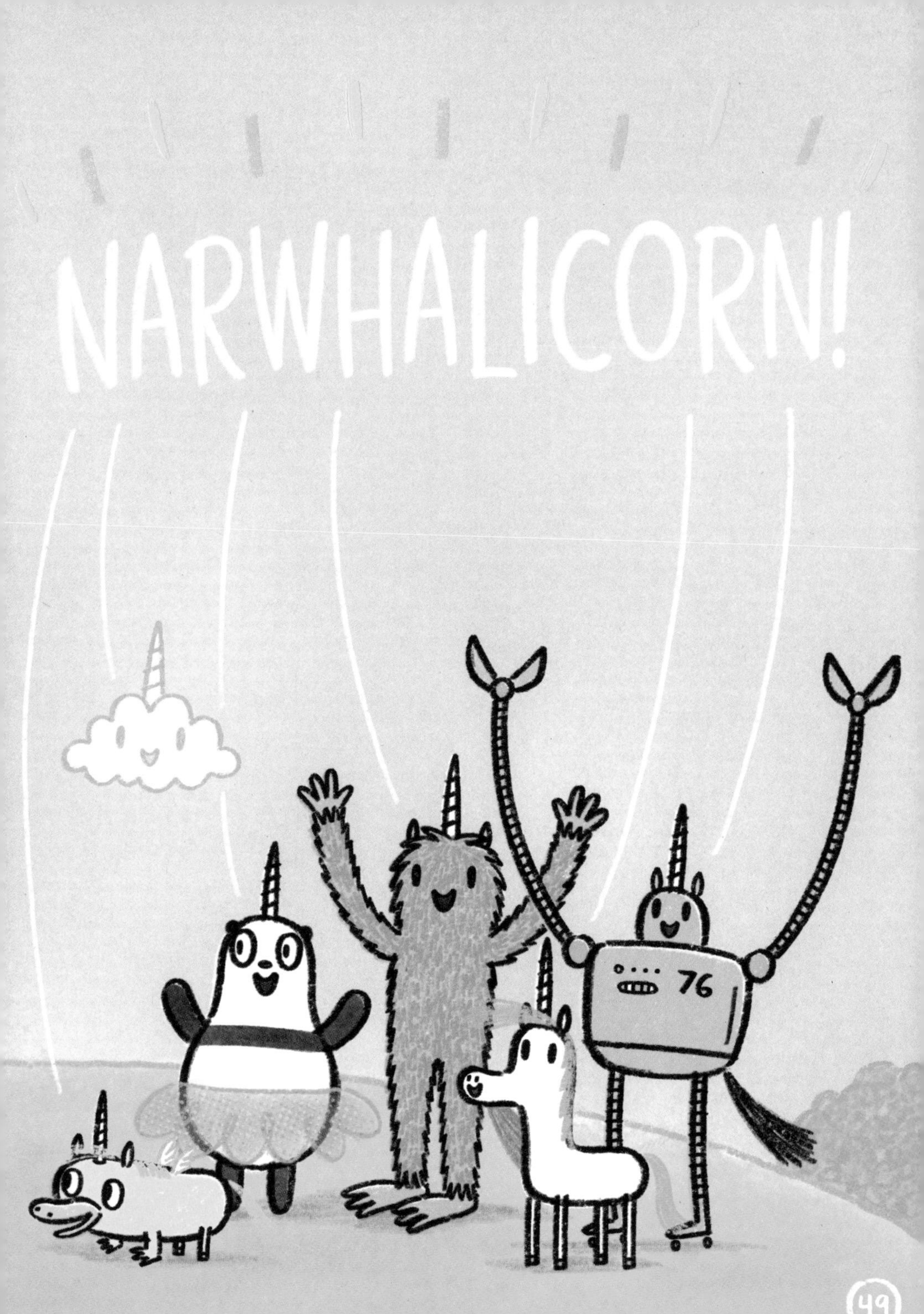
NARWHALICORN!
76

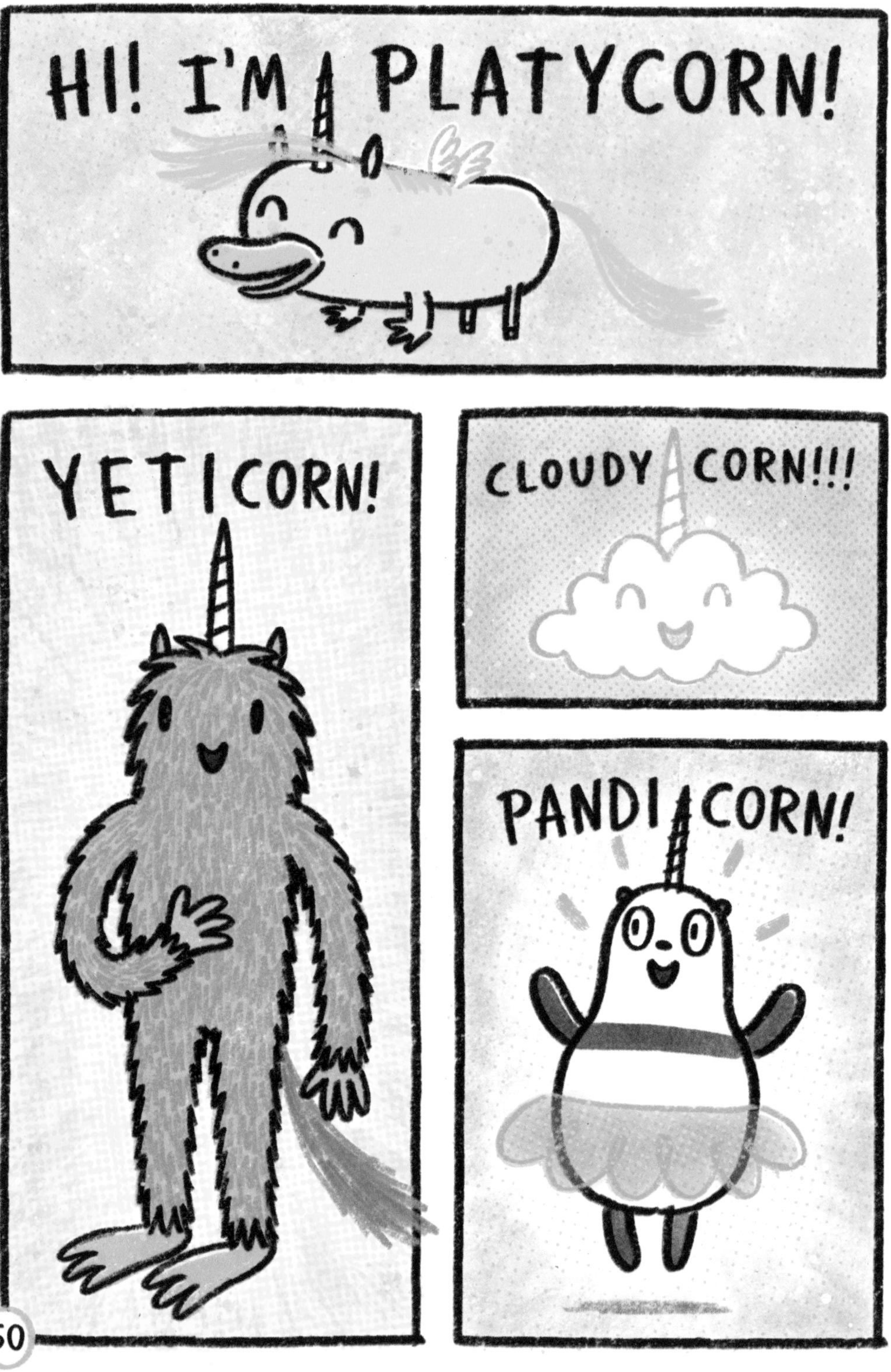
HI! I'M A PLATYCORN!
YETICORN!
CLOUDY CORN!!!
PANDICORN!

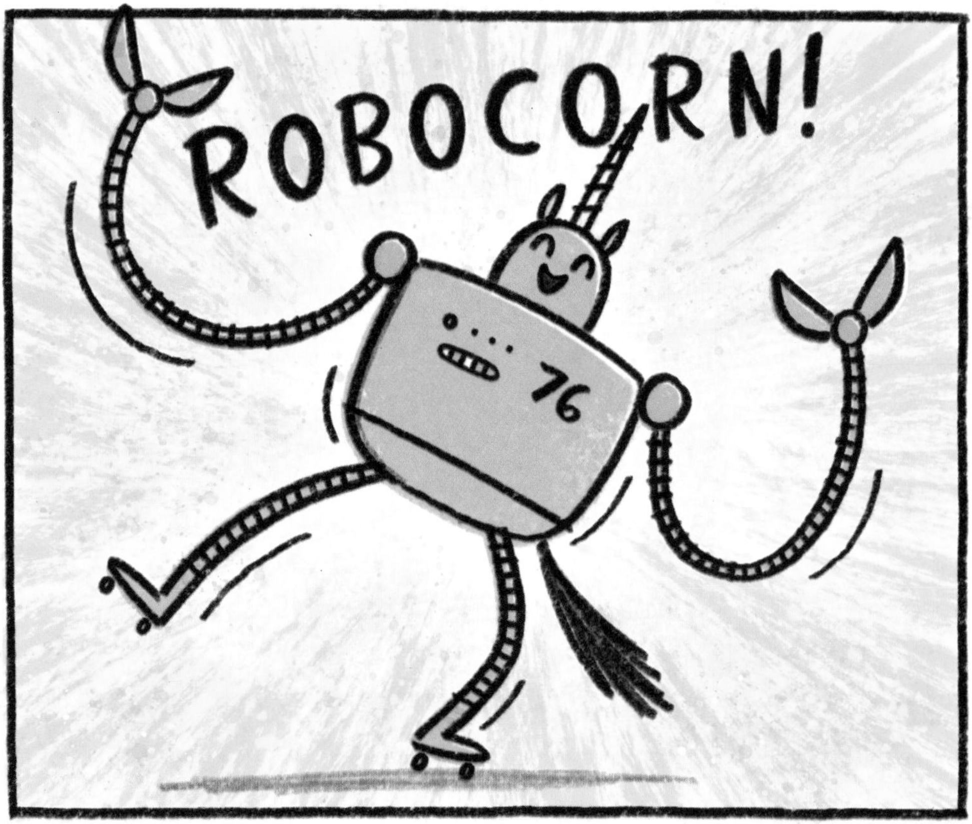
ROBOCORN!
76

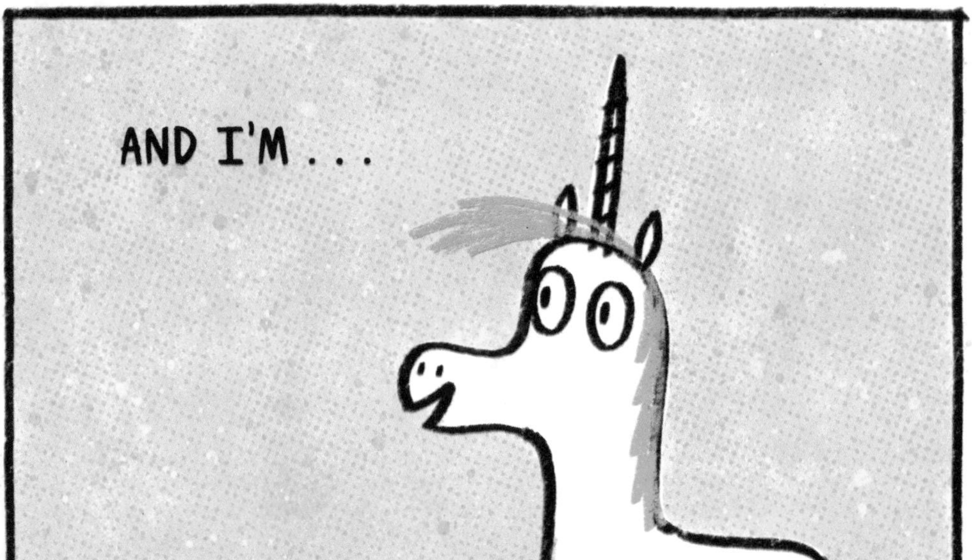
AND I'M . . .

HORSICORN!

WELCOME TO THE
UNICORN PLANET!
WHERE EVERYONE IS
A UNICORN!

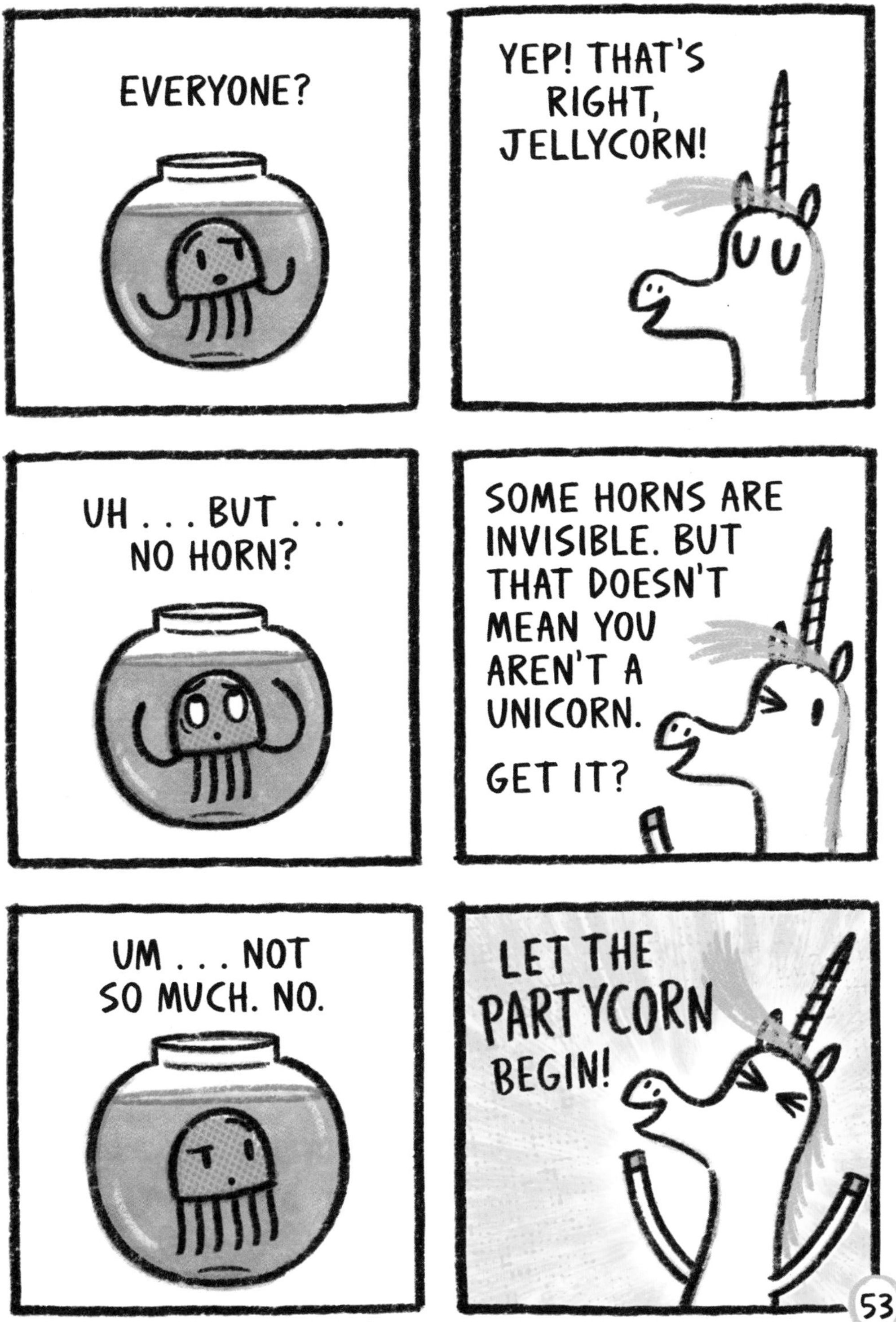
EVERYONE?
YEP! THAT'S RIGHT, JELLYCORN!
UH . . . BUT . . . NO HORN?
SOME HORNS ARE INVISIBLE. BUT THAT DOESN'T MEAN YOU AREN'T A UNICORN.
GET IT?
UM . . . NOT SO MUCH. NO.
LET THE PARTYCORN BEGIN!

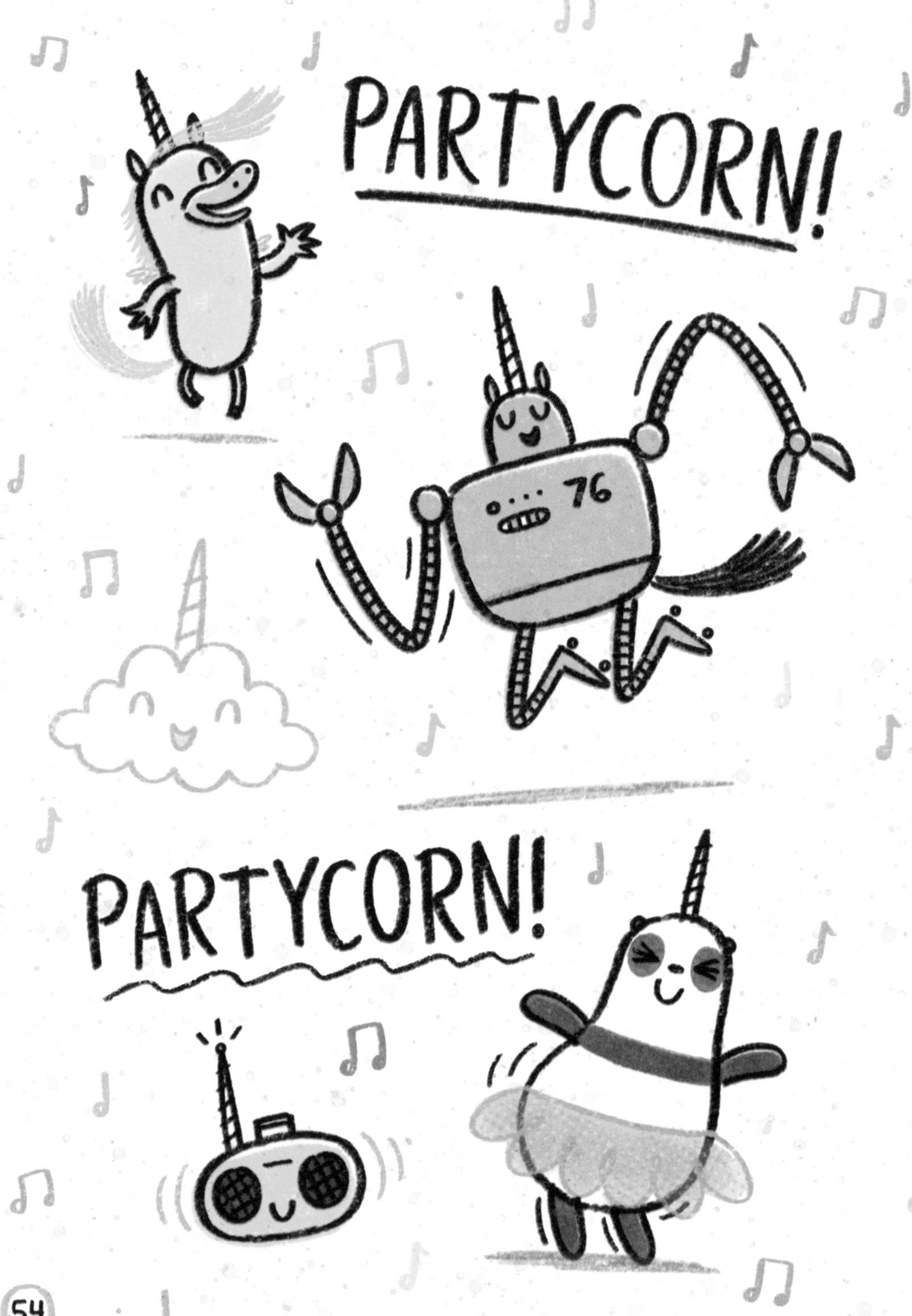
PARTYCORN!
76
PARTYCORN!

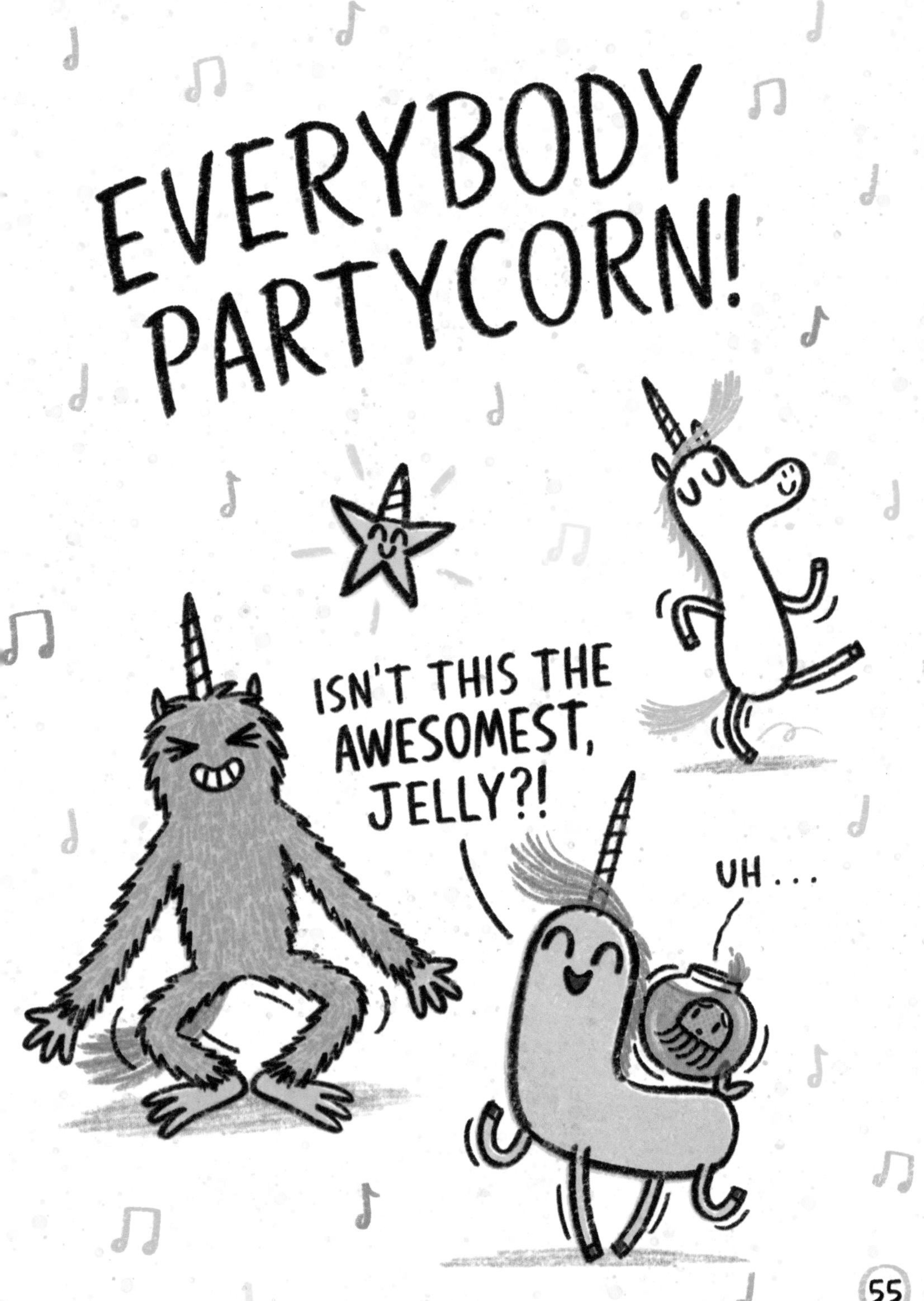
EVERYBODY PARTYCORN!
ISN'T THIS THE AWESOMEST, JELLY?!
UH . . .

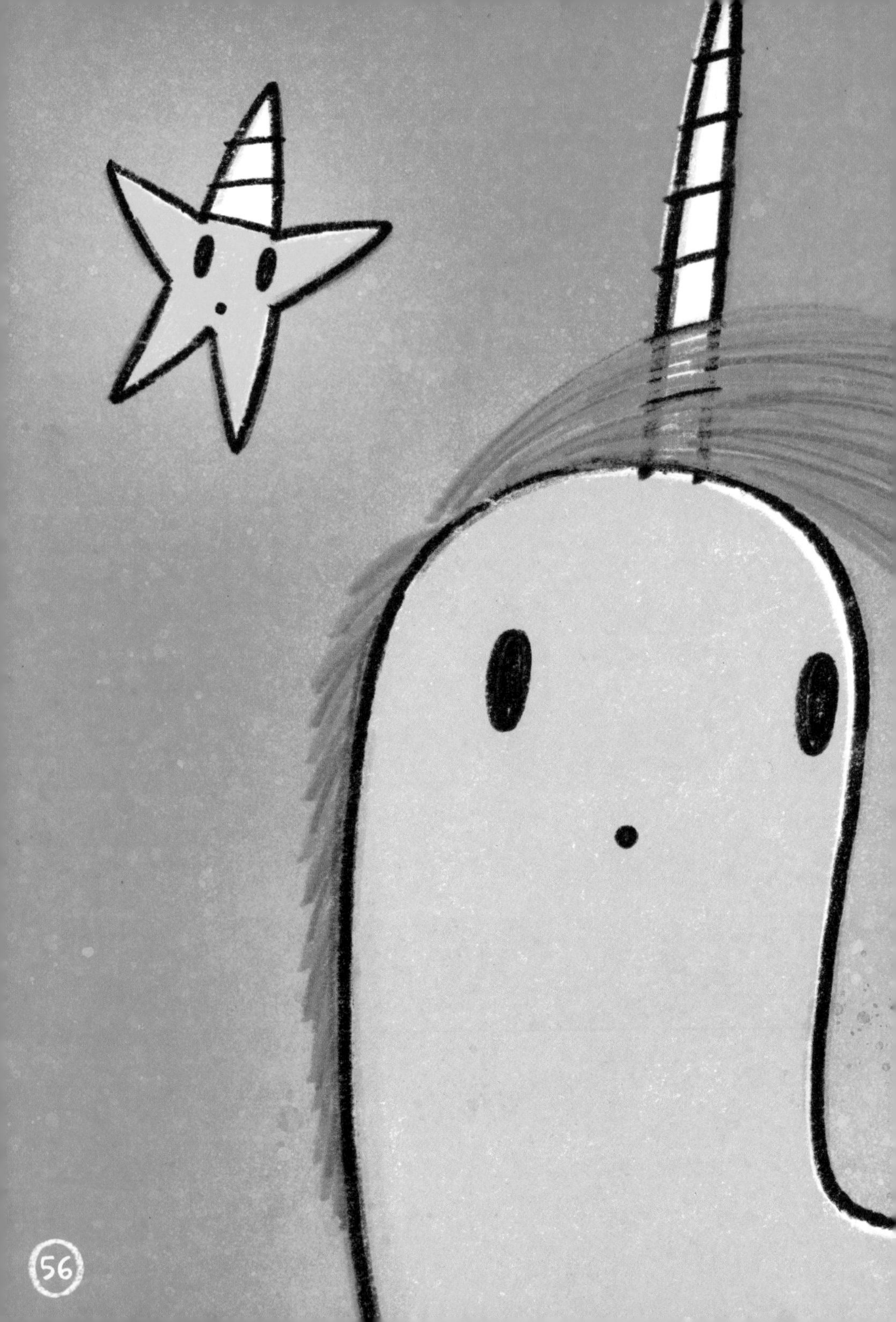

NO! IT'S NOT!

NOT FOR ME, AT LEAST. ALL NIGHT I'VE BEEN SUPER SLEEPY AND FELT LIKE A JELLYFISH OUT OF WATER. I'VE BEEN TRYING TO TELL YOU THIS IS ALL TOO OUT-THERE FOR ME TONIGHT.

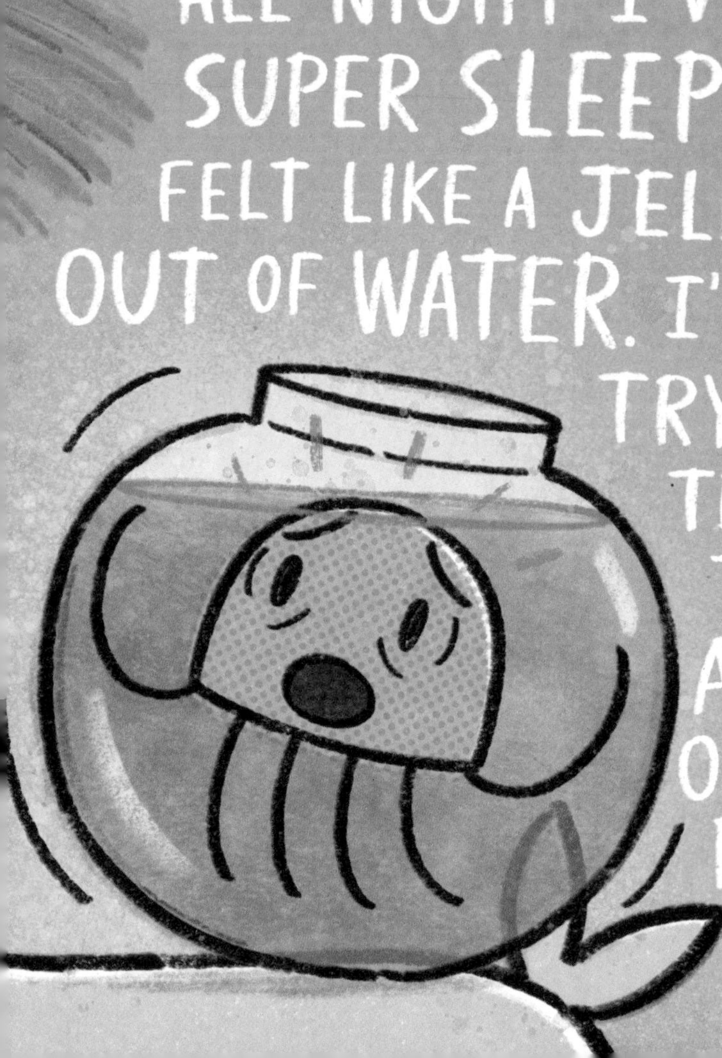

I JUST WISH
I COULD GO HOME...

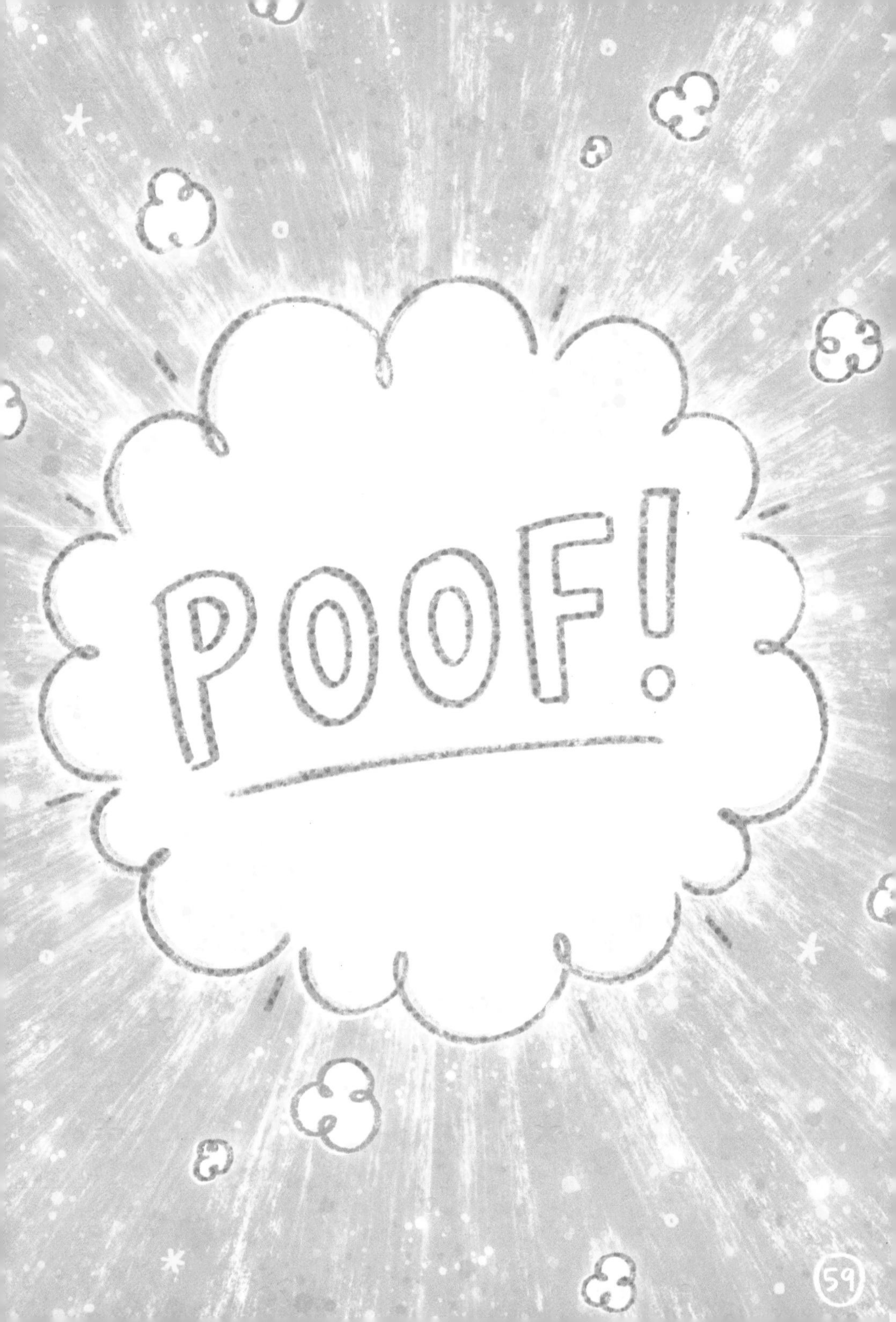
POOF!

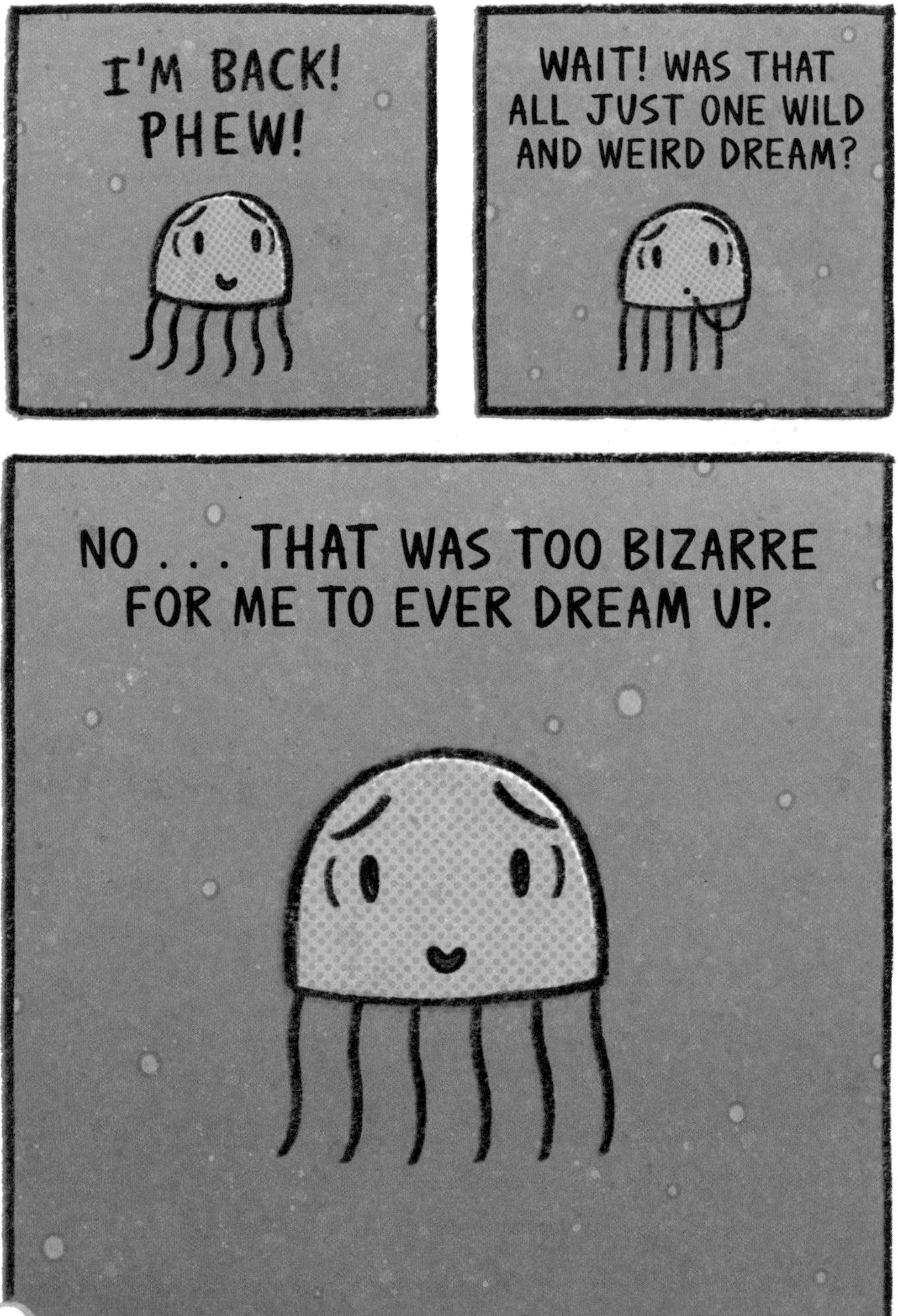
I'M BACK! PHEW!
WAIT! WAS THAT ALL JUST ONE WILD AND WEIRD DREAM?
NO . . . THAT WAS TOO BIZARRE FOR ME TO EVER DREAM UP.

NARWHALICORN SURE
SEEMED HAPPY UP THERE.

I WONDER IF THEY'LL
EVER COME HOME . . .

MEANWHILE, BACK ON THE UNICORN PLANET . . .

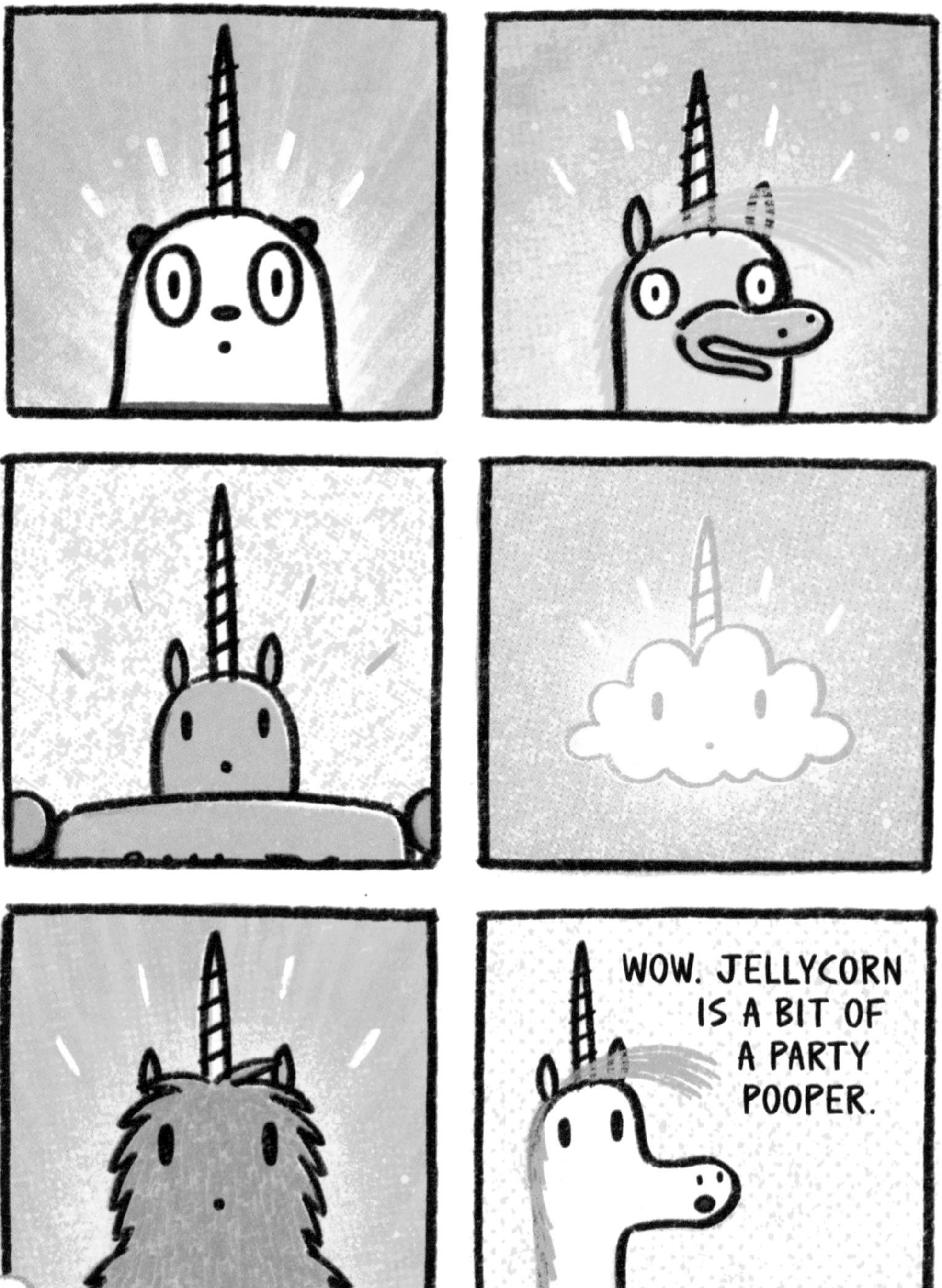

WOW. JELLYCORN IS A BIT OF A PARTY POOPER.

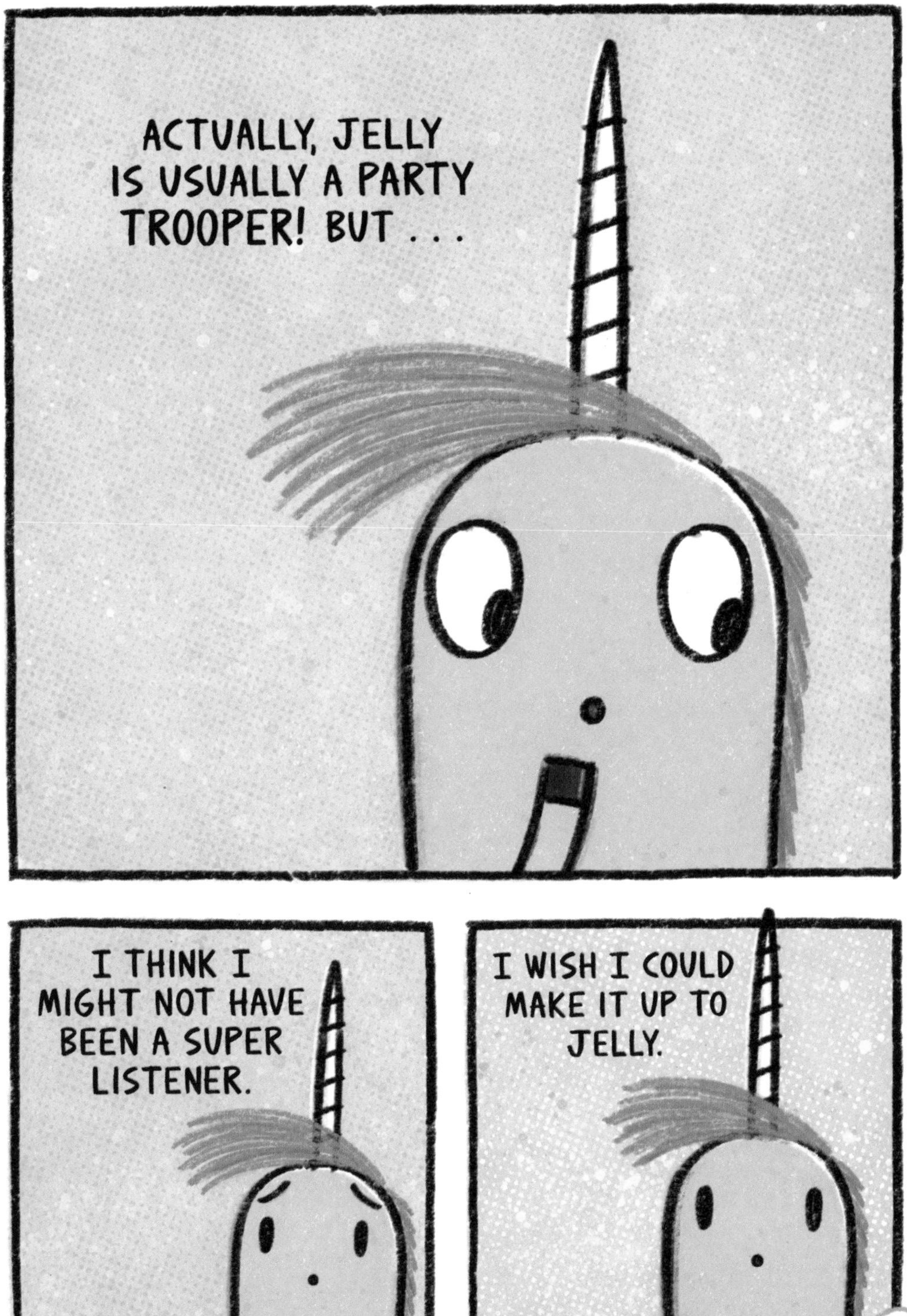
ACTUALLY, JELLY IS USUALLY A PARTY TROOPER! BUT . . .
I THINK I MIGHT NOT HAVE BEEN A SUPER LISTENER.
I WISH I COULD MAKE IT UP TO JELLY.

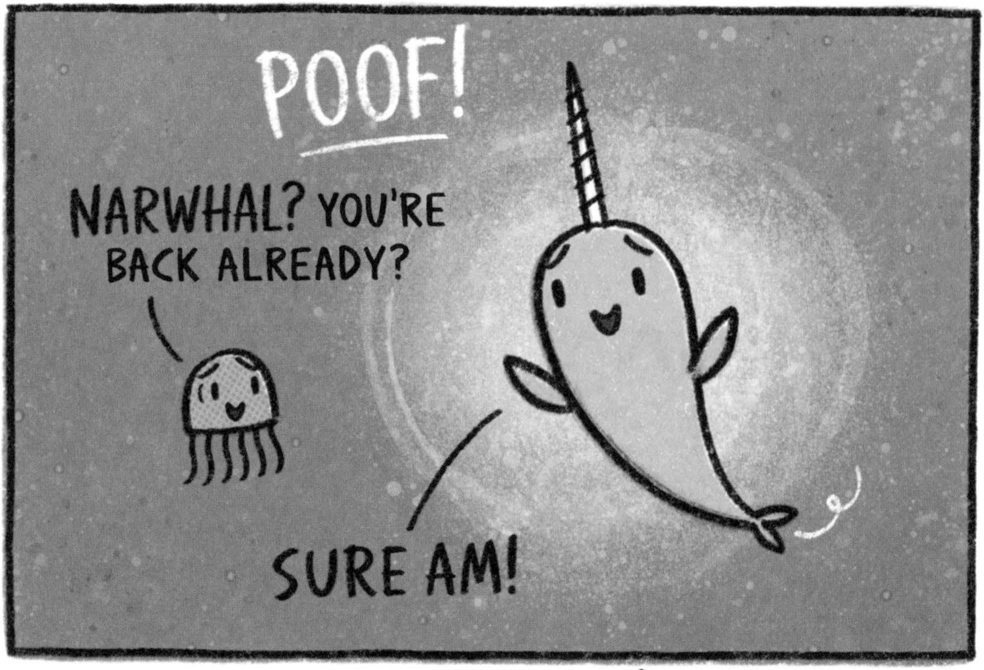
POOF!
NARWHAL? YOU'RE BACK ALREADY?
SURE AM!

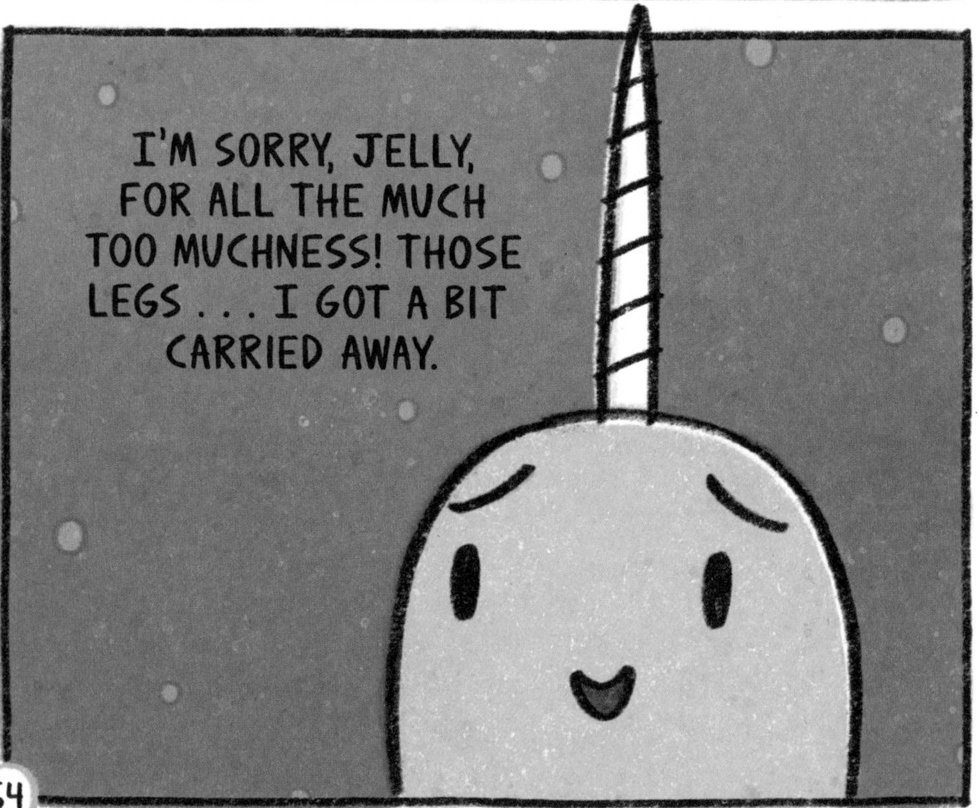
I'M SORRY, JELLY, FOR ALL THE MUCH TOO MUCHNESS! THOSE LEGS . . . I GOT A BIT CARRIED AWAY.

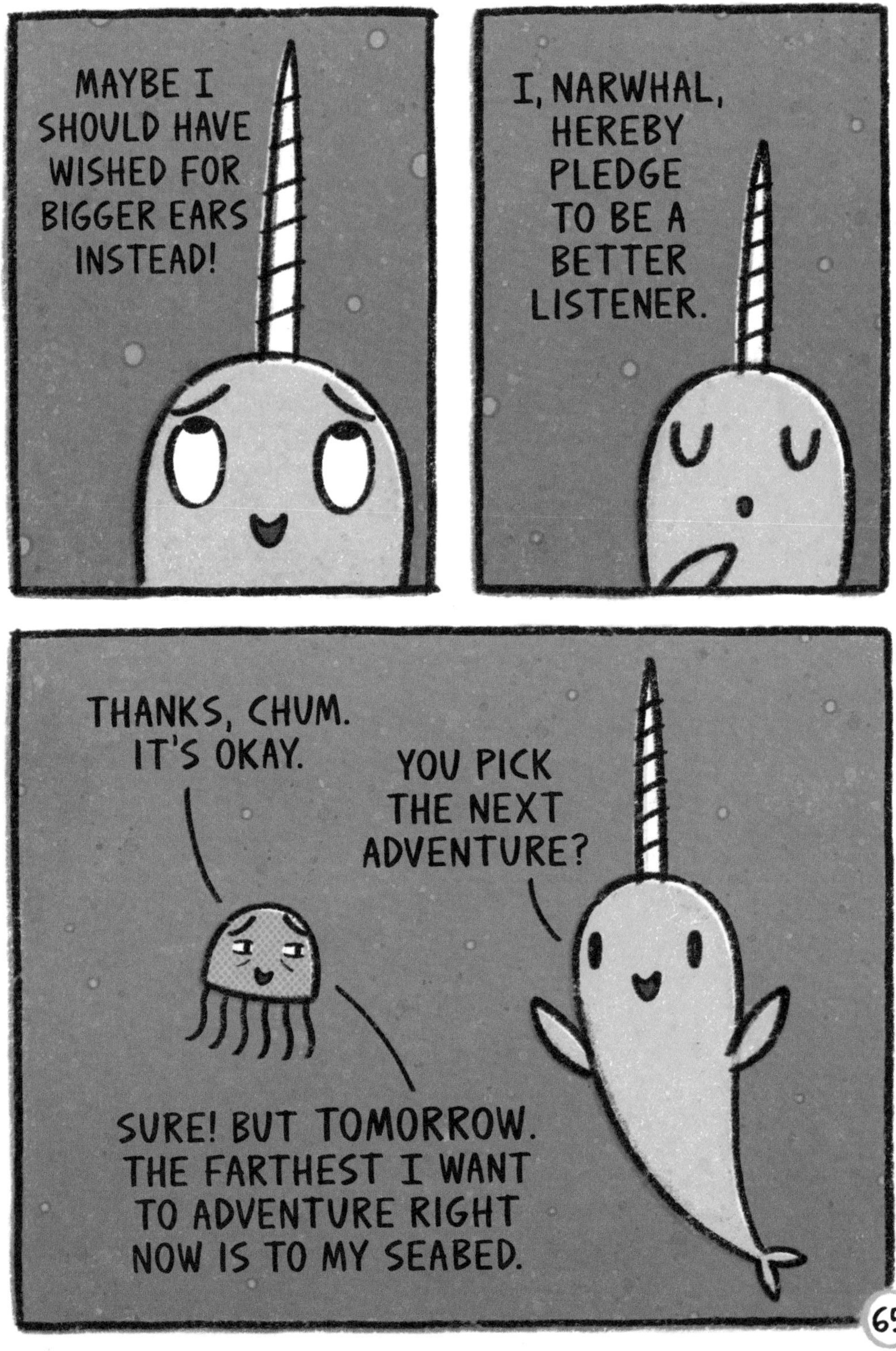
MAYBE I SHOULD HAVE WISHED FOR BIGGER EARS INSTEAD!
I, NARWHAL, HEREBY PLEDGE TO BE A BETTER LISTENER.
THANKS, CHUM. IT'S OKAY.
YOU PICK THE NEXT ADVENTURE?
SURE! BUT TOMORROW. THE FARTHEST I WANT TO ADVENTURE RIGHT NOW IS TO MY SEABED.

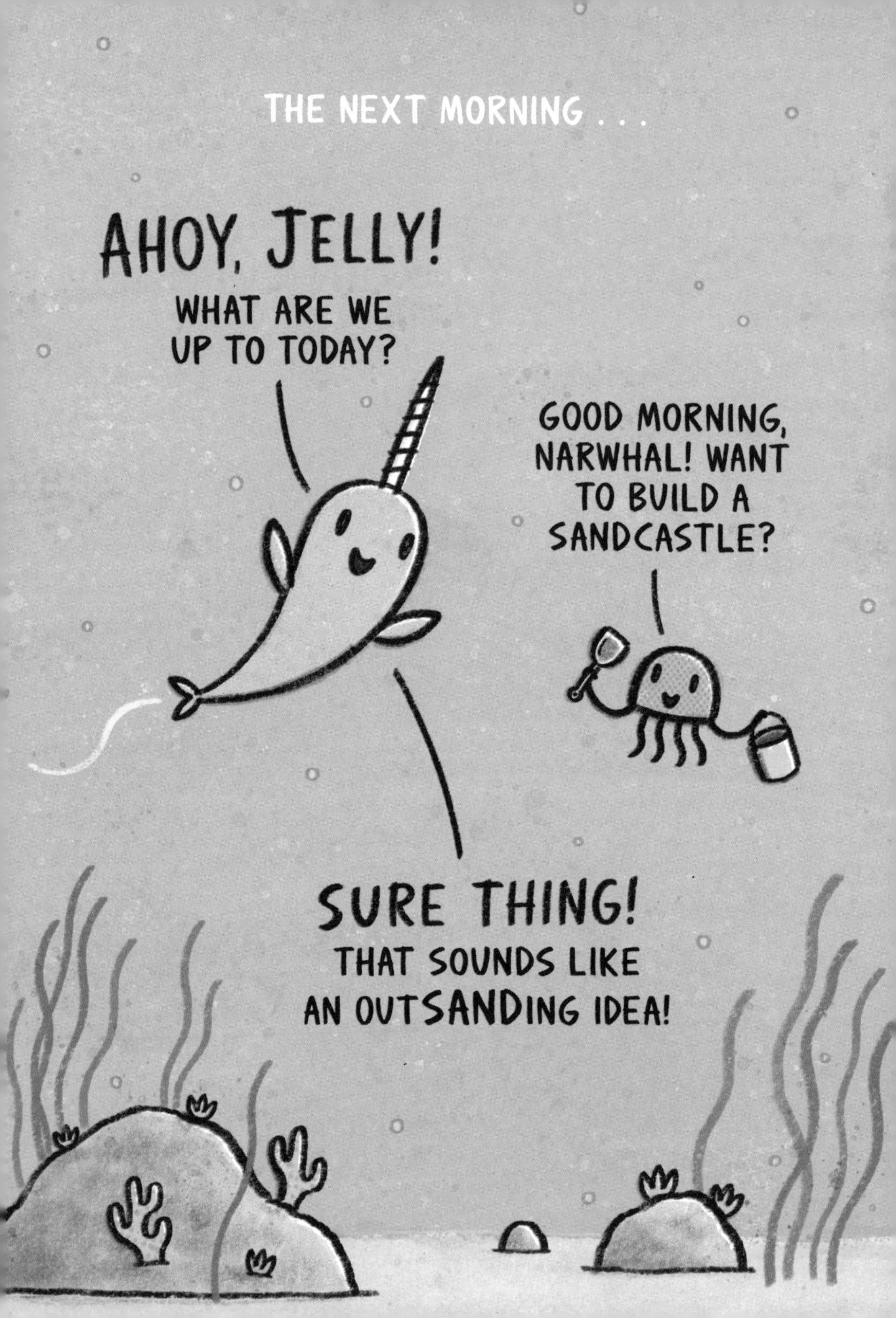
THE NEXT MORNING . . .
AHOY, JELLY!
WHAT ARE WE UP TO TODAY?
GOOD MORNING, NARWHAL! WANT TO BUILD A SANDCASTLE?
SURE THING!
THAT SOUNDS LIKE AN OUTSANDING IDEA!

A LITTLE WHILE LATER . . .

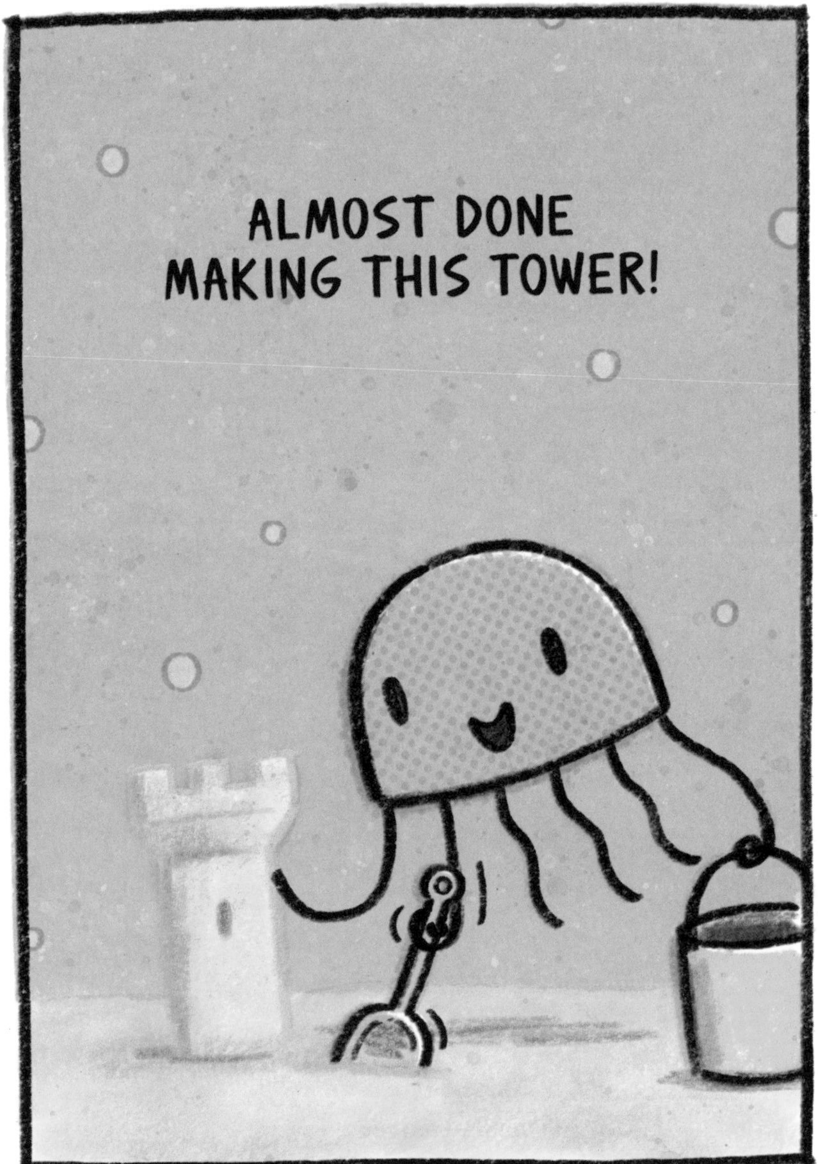
ALMOST DONE MAKING THIS TOWER!

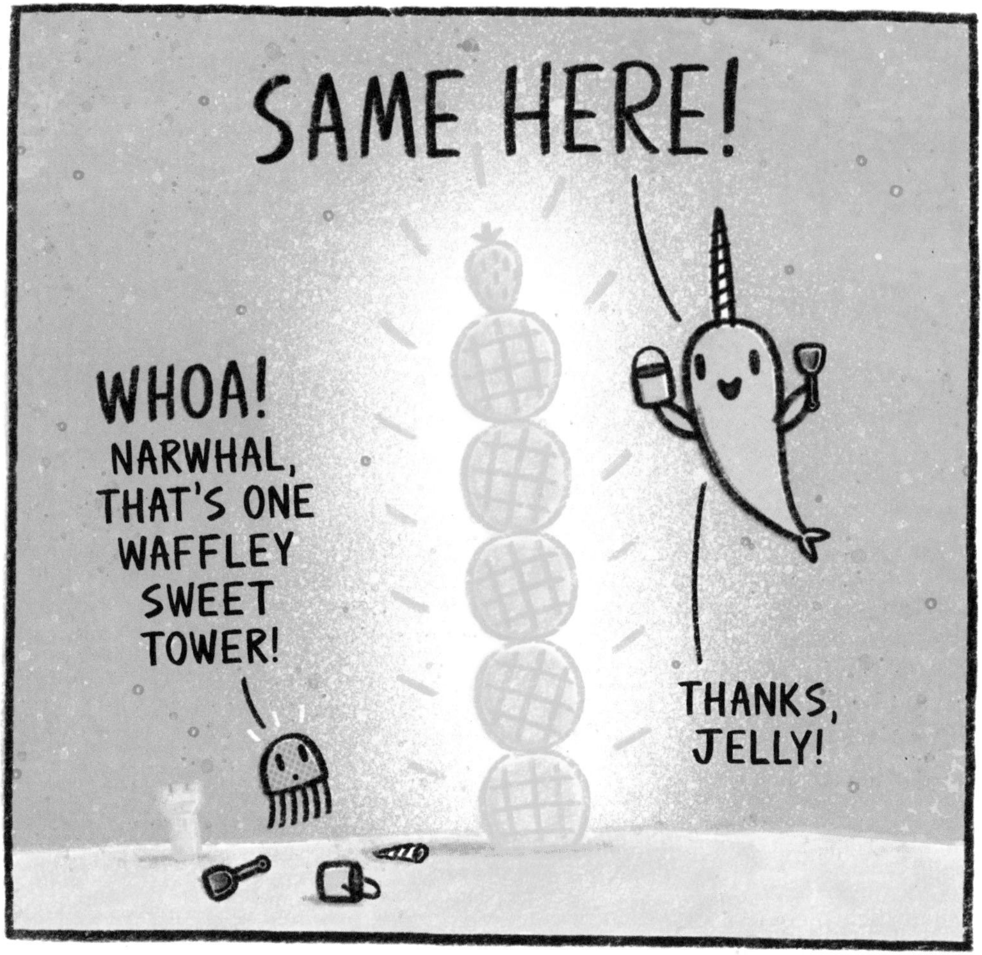
SAME HERE!
WHOA! NARWHAL, THAT'S ONE WAFFLEY SWEET TOWER!
THANKS, JELLY!

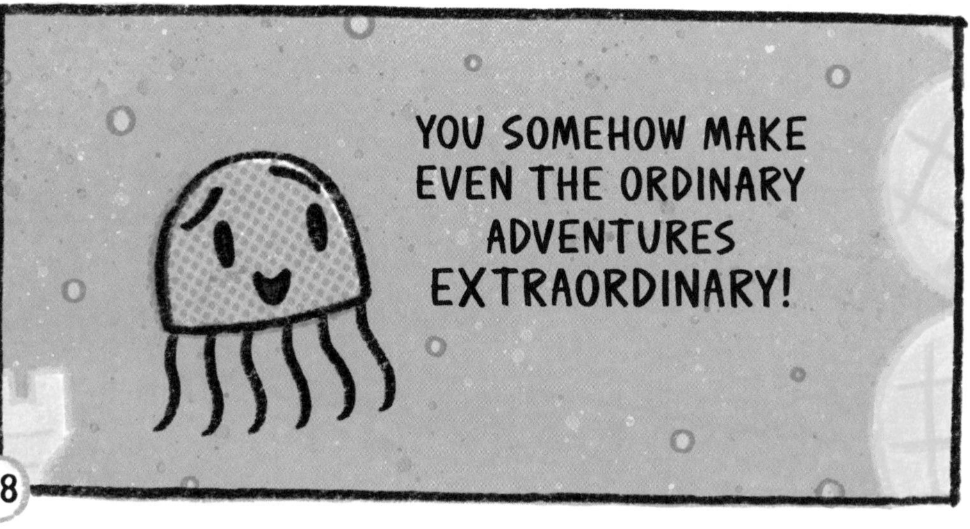
YOU SOMEHOW MAKE EVEN THE ORDINARY ADVENTURES EXTRAORDINARY!

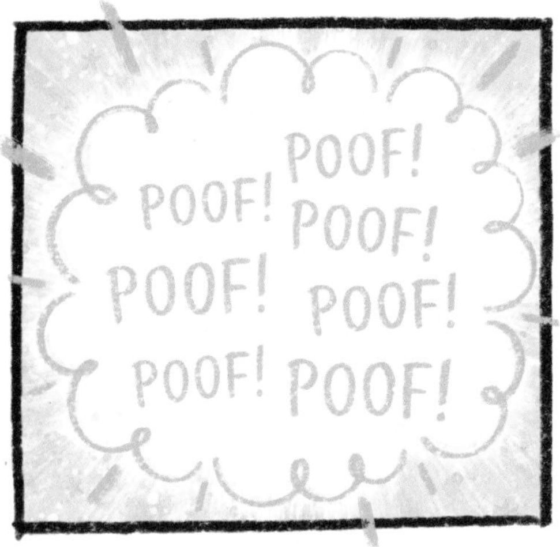
POOF! POOF!
POOF! POOF!
POOF! POOF!
POOF! POOF!

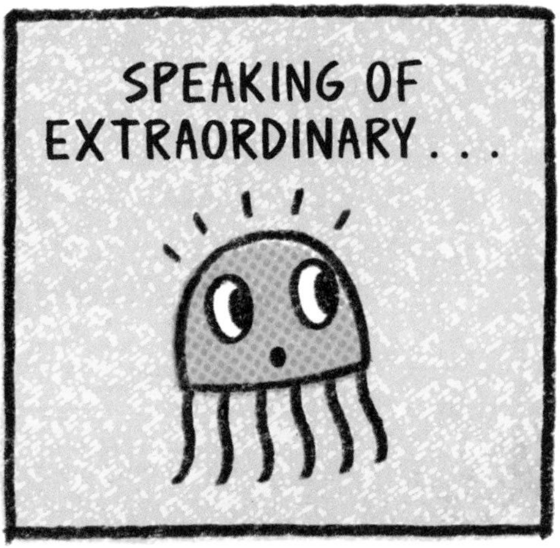
SPEAKING OF EXTRAORDINARY . . .

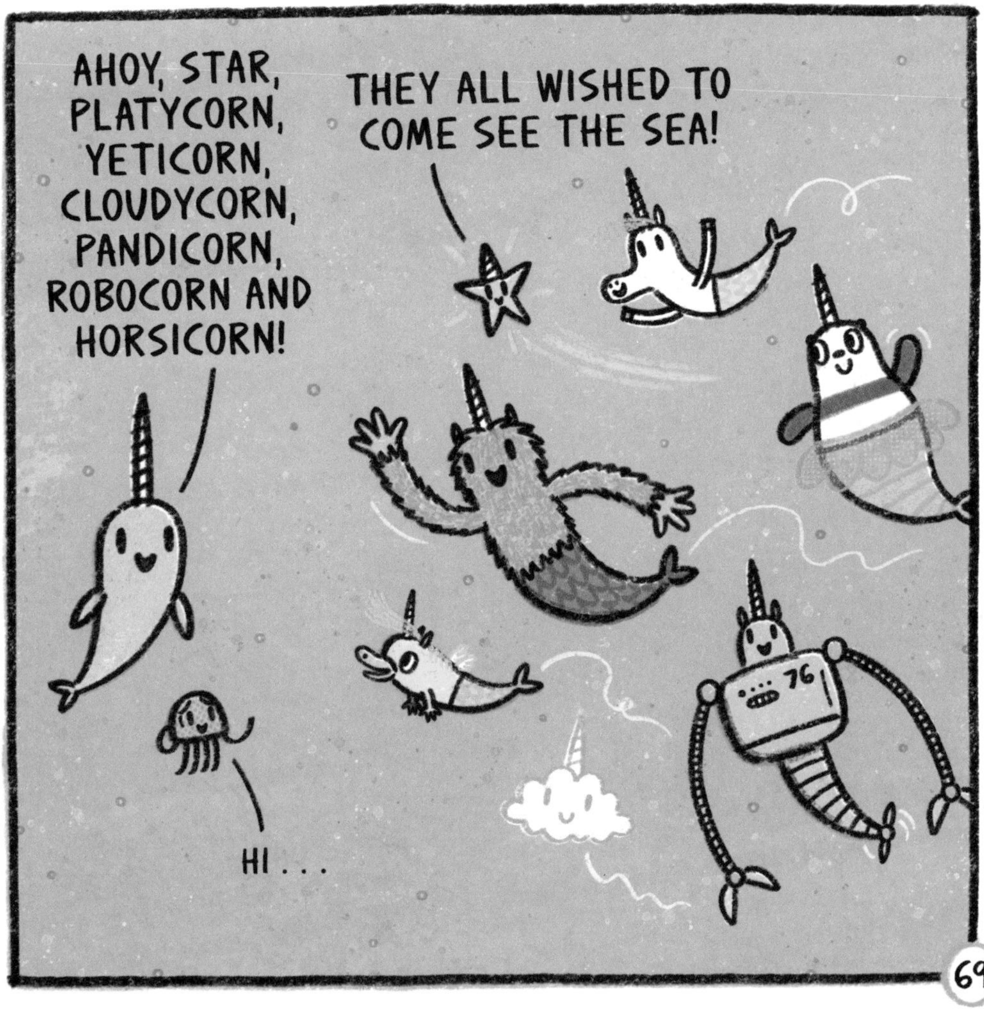
AHOY, STAR, PLATYCORN, YETICORN, CLOUDYCORN, PANDICORN, ROBOCORN AND HORSICORN!
THEY ALL WISHED TO COME SEE THE SEA!
HI . . .
76

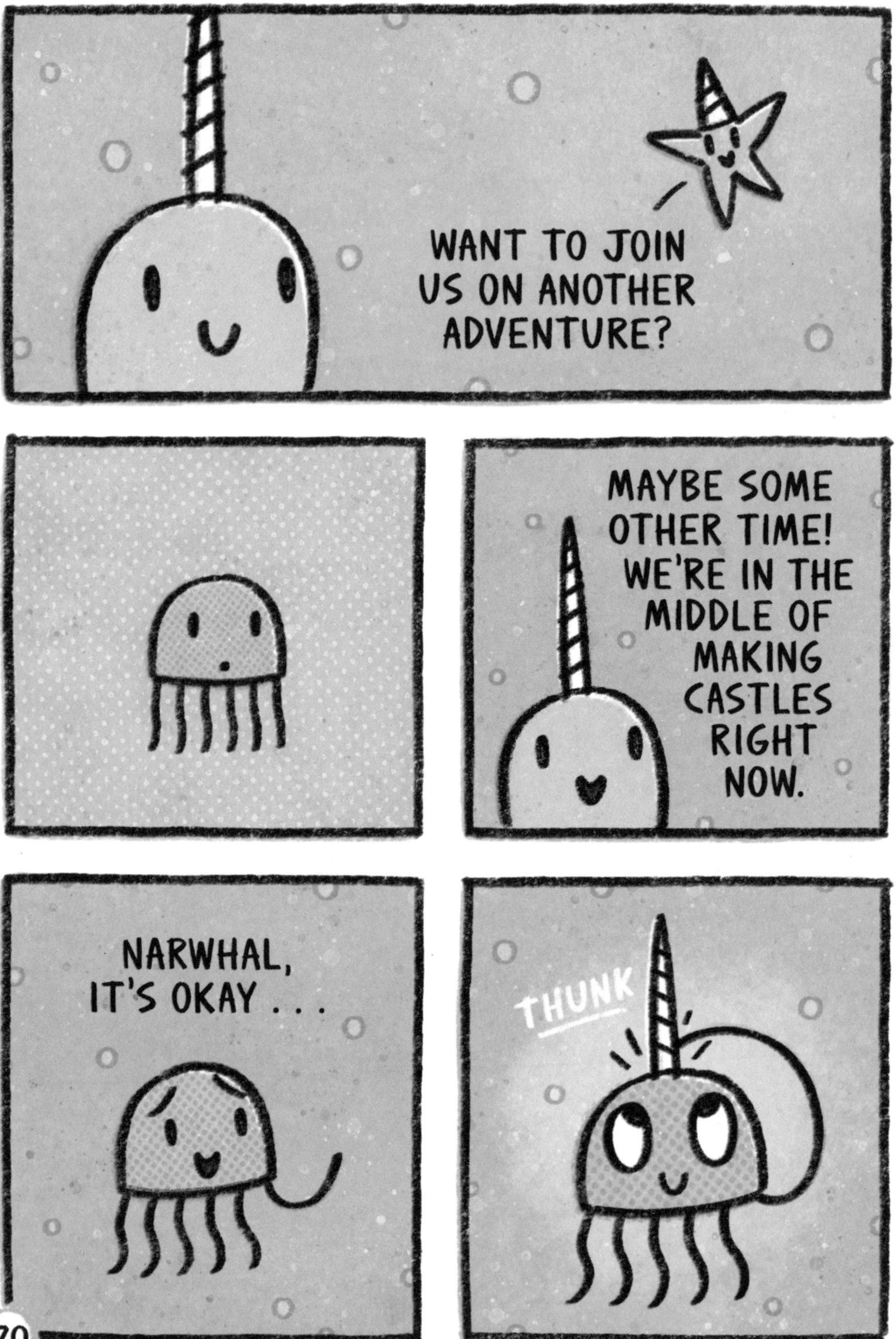
WANT TO JOIN US ON ANOTHER ADVENTURE?
MAYBE SOME OTHER TIME! WE'RE IN THE MIDDLE OF MAKING CASTLES RIGHT NOW.
NARWHAL, IT'S OKAY . . .
THUNK

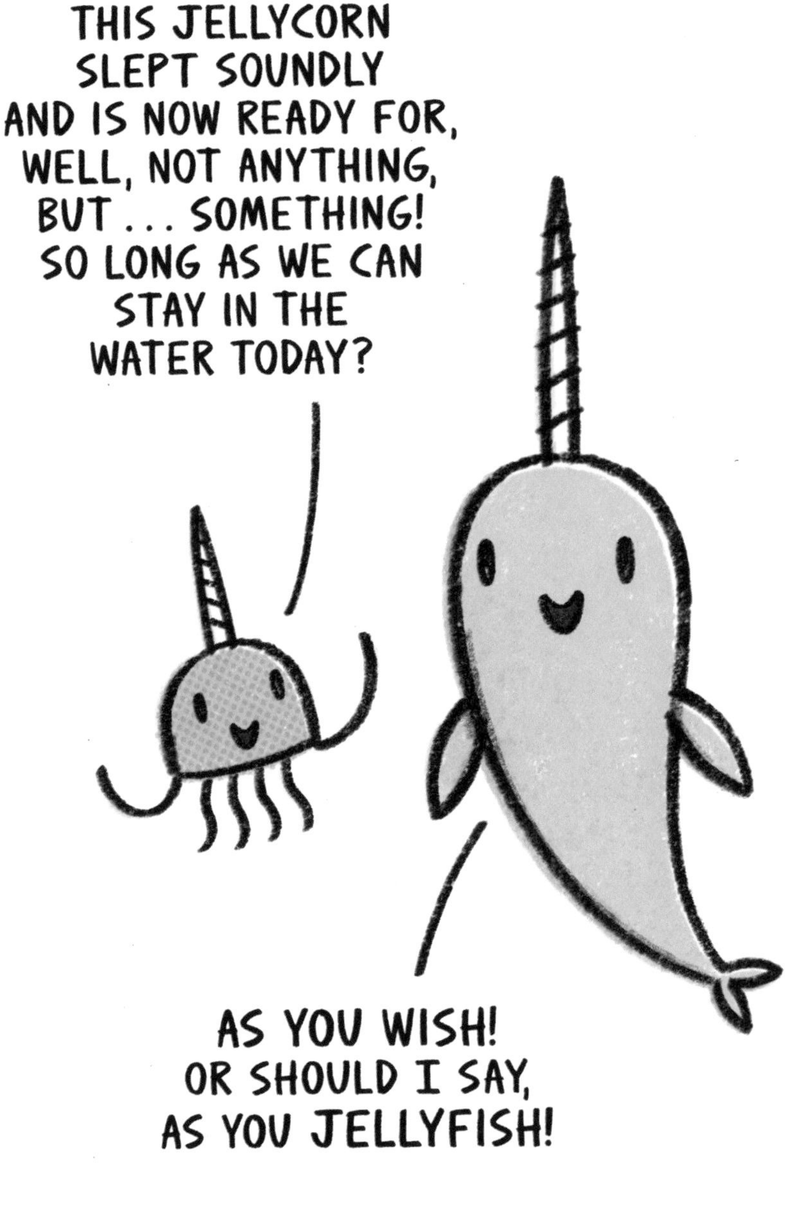
THIS JELLYCORN SLEPT SOUNDLY AND IS NOW READY FOR, WELL, NOT ANYTHING, BUT . . . SOMETHING! SO LONG AS WE CAN STAY IN THE WATER TODAY?
AS YOU WISH! OR SHOULD I SAY, AS YOU JELLYFISH!

PARTYCORN!
PARTYCORN!

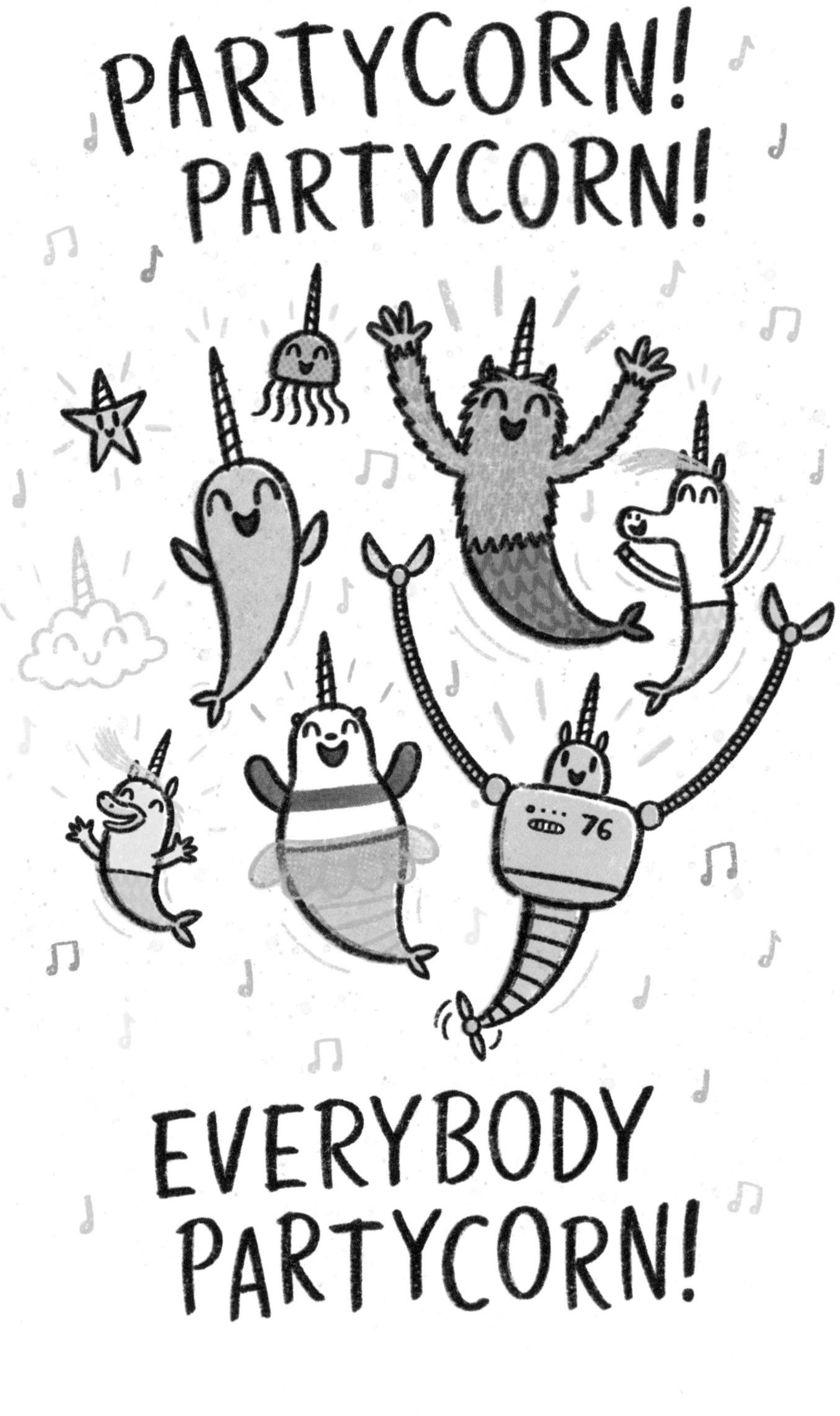
76

EVERYBODY
PARTYCORN!

MORE NARWHAL AND JELLY

ADVENTURES
COMING SOON!

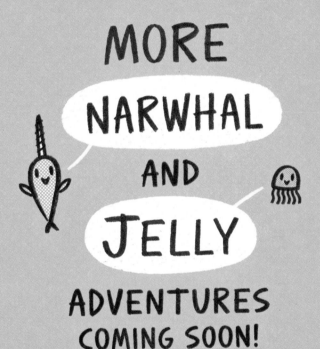